KORSONILOFF

korsoniloff

Matt Cohen

ANANSI 1969

House of Anansi Press
671 Spadina Avenue
Toronto 179, Ontario

Manufactured in Canada

I

Korsoniloff, André Korsoniloff, in an off-white gabardine trench-coat, a more definitely grey cowled sweatshirt, jockey underwear, blue pinstriped trousers, nondescript socks, last summer's rained-on cardboard suede shoes, making his way up Avenue Road in Toronto on a sunny April morning

The mood is spiritual poverty. It was compulsory so he assumed it. An undefined guilt stretching both ways in time

Korsoniloff finds his shoulders beginning to move around in the trench-coat, establishing their size and territory, trying to feel his stomach's flatness by contacting the fuzzy sweat-shirt inside at sundry vertical points, feet powering his walk through the warped rubber of the leftover shoes, endlessly initiating the recapitulation of his physicality so that

In space and time. Too quickly, the child is the father of to the man. A stitch in

The summer sun inside-outside lay across the bed exposing the air and the breeze plays through it so the boy lies in the sun feeling it wondering if it is a magic carpet which could float him outside-inside anywhere although just lying there suspended with the dust particles and feeling the current move through his body is enough and wonders does it really move through or does it just feel that way

Lying suspended, half-formed thoughts dissolving in the warm morning, time floats like a nowhere tide but how long can you can anyone stay in that world in

If you feel your toes against the sheets it's alright but if you have to hold their weight and the blankets too with just the nails' edges then it's time to cut your toenails. Which was the case that inside-outside morning and the boy thought briefly if he should cut them and then return. But once he was up it wouldn't be the same, anyhow you can't just cut toenails. If you do they break and spray fragments and the edge comes out ragged and scratchy at night which means that the thing to do is to walk to the bathroom and then put one foot into the bathtub with the water going lukewarm till the nails get mushy or at least soft and can be sliced clean and neat (to avoid all this he had once tried filing them but gotten bored)

The incident on the dock was

In a white house remarkable for its appearance of great size, piled up upon itself, squeezed into porches at the edges, as if built in a game by some playful giant who, not quite satisfied when finished, gave it a boot in the ass and left it to find its own occupants

So when Ivan Mikhail Khorosanilov (his name bastardised but only partly by a recalcitrant immigration official whose wife in sickbed read Oblomov and heard rumours of Dostoyevsky) reached the house after sundry wanderings through upstate New York and finally into Canada and then north up the Ottawa River following a job teaching school he found it empty and big enough to contain his dreams.

But Mikhail it's so big.

So?

And it needs so much work . . . it's so far from the school.

So it was settled and they moved in accepting the mutual challenge, Ivan Mikhail coming home from school each night, the first two miles walking letting the day drain through him, then by the time he was home obsessed by two more miles of trying to decide what to do with this amorphous wooden chaos, throwing off his coat in the front hall (the door isn't hung properly, it sticks, it will be drafty in the winter) going into the kitchen (the stove is smoking again maybe it's the chimney, the draft is open full) but finally going up to the room with his tools and working on the window (nothing's square, how will it ever close or open without sticking?). The room for the child, the first child, who must begin in conquered territory, his (her?) birth only two months away and only the roof is fixed

Feeling his thighs against the cloth of his pants Korsoniloff is suddenly reminded of being inside Marie, of her thighs pressed around him, of her smile which at first he thought looked different only because of the angle but then realised that it was a different smile, possibly even a mystical smile of ultimate connection . . . but he hadn't seen that smile for almost a year, seen it live, seen it as anything but an image surprising him on the street or interrupting him just as he was about to fall asleep. Marie. Her upside-down smile constituted the particulars of his abyss

The boy stretched and contemplated murder. There was a spring fly, slow and soundless, making its way from his dresser to the window (you'll never know what I went through to fix that window his father had told him), but his limbs were still suspended in dreams and he settled back into the pillow reaching reaching

5

A month before the baby was due Ivan Mikhail was finishing the window, scraping off the putty (he'd had to replace the pane, which had been broken in a fit of temper two days before) with a razor blade and wiping the edges clean with a cloth when Anna called from downstairs.

I've called the doctor, it's starting . . .

What's starting?

The baby, you idiot.

My god, thought Mikhail, what if it's twins? There's only one window. He gave the glass a final swish and ran downstairs. Don't move, he shouted, whatever you do don't move.

When Mikhail got downstairs she was standing in the kitchen, looking out the window and drumming her fingers on her belly. I don't know, she said, I don't know. It's so early

On an April Sunday morning Korsoniloff, André, proceeding orderly in a northward direction, senses the spring and recollects the mood of his affair with Marie. Spread before him, panoramically, a stretch of lawn preceded by a row of yellow daffodils presents itself for his inspection.

Then like a framed picture from a woman's magazine, Korsoniloff perceives caught in the sunlight against a stonewall church the great wedding scene. The bride's white, the perfection of the choreography, catches his eye and as he stares mesmerized the bride becomes Marie.

Seized by the moment, caught in the interstices of time, so aware that the moment is a snapshot memory, Korsoniloff undertook to reorient his spatial surroundings. More specifically he bent over and severed seven yellow daffodils to carry towards the wedding party which

The boy reached over the side of the bed and picked up

the photograph. She was dark and slim, he knew she must be slim, his mother (his 'real' mother he sometimes thought, to differentiate her from Bess who was most definitely not his real mother). He looked at the photograph, entering his own communion with it—and was still in her presence when Bess shouted to him, dissolving the morning, the moment, to come down to breakfast. He put on his jeans and running shoes and started looking

Seven golden daffodils, arcane mandala for a confluent yellow morning, borne by Korsoniloff towards Marie. He sees her look up, suddenly aware of his approach but not startled, smile pleased for the camera, the morning, and perhaps, guessing what Korsoniloff has not yet understood about his own action, the impending restoration of her own innocence. Accepting the invitation of her smile Korsoniloff continued and edged in beside her so that the photographer might preserve the presentation.

With the click of the camera Marie (later he thought it must have set off some unexpected memory of their nights) moved back, looking almost afraid. Korsoniloff, following her motion and realizing that she must have sensed the nature of his gift, was suddenly filled with tenderness. Accompanied by an exuberance at this climacteric of her gratitude so that the outstretched flowers were carried, delicate fragrant mandala, direct to her face. And as the petals collapsed, singly and together, Korsoniloff felt a hand

When his father told him (André come outside with me) that he was getting married again (you'll be meeting her tomorrow night) he had asked André if he remembered Anna and given him a framed photograph (taken just after we were married). They were sitting outside, on the railing of one of

the squeezed-out porches, talking, and André had a terrible
tension in his stomach—not a new feeling but a magni-
fication of something that was already there. (She was
very beautiful, we used to sit here sometimes and watch
the sunset) and André pressed the photograph against his
stomach where it hurt, hardly able to hear the words (I know
you and Bess will get along) until the tension spread through
his whole body, buzzing and numbing, filling his mind and
blocking all sound

There was really no question or doubt. After two hours
the nurse (secretary, assistant, midwife) came down for more
water and Mikhail knew that there was really no doubt at
all. Still, he waited, not asking, because waiting was the thing
for him to do and maybe if he waited long and painfully
enough everything would be alright but really he knew it
wasn't and wouldn't be.

Finally exhausted by his unhabitual stoicism. Mikhail
fell asleep on the couch. Mail order? Church auction? No, a
former minister's couch passed on to the previous teacher
and thence to Mikhail as a parting gift, a flowered consolation
prize. So when the doctor came in and announced one healthy
boy and one tired but alive mother Mikhail awoke from his
unremembered dreams already mourning

Spun around to face the groom Korsoniloff, never violent
and always paralysed, felt his other shoulder tensed in un-
familiar synchronisation; his flowered hand suddenly came into
his line of vision, his body twisted, following the daffodils,
until they met the face of the man in the white carnation falling

II

At the police station Korsoniloff made his phonecall.
Alex Tonker, college fatman turned lawyer. He had been in
and out of the periphery of Korsoniloff's awareness over a
decade ago. Attraction by repulsion. Big, unsure, gregarious in
an edgily obscene sort of way, he gave the impression

May I speak to Alex Tonker?
Who's speaking please?
André Korsoniloff.
Just one moment.
Hello Tonker? This is Korsoniloff, André Korsoniloff
speaking . . . Fine thank you. Actually, I wanted to see you
professionally. No, I'm at the station now. I'm not sure what
I'm charged with; I didn't ask. No, I didn't do anything
unusual; I was out walking today . . .

Korsoniloff, encaged, alternately paced, lay on his bed,
and worried about his constipation. In one of the prone
periods, wishing it was summer so he could count the flies on
the ceiling, he became aware of ponderous footsteps moving
down the corridor towards his cell. Accompanying them was

9

the sharper sound of the guard, so when the door was opened
and Tonker stepped in Korsoniloff was already anticipating him.

Tonker came into the cell, ignoring Korsoniloff's hand,
and sat down on the bunk chewing his cheek and looking at
Korsoniloff as if he'd been caught shoplifting nylons.

He had once been fat. Now he was immense. His flesh
was arranged

Now look here Korsoniloff, you're charged with disorderly conduct. You understand what that means don't you?
Making a public nuisance of yourself. I suggest you just pay
the goddam fine and forget it.

What if I don't pay the fine?

The fine is fifty goddam dollars at most.

Tonker pulled three chocolate marshmallow cookies
from his jacket pocket and gulped them down.

You wouldn't have any pop here? Never mind. Now
look, why don't you just put up the goddam bail and we'll
come down in a couple of days and settle the whole thing.
You can take me out to lunch afterwards—you look hungry.

What am I charged with exactly?

What you're charged with exactly is disorderly conduct

Tonker coming drunk to Korsoniloff's room at the
university, flopping down on the bed and, pointing his finger
at Korsoniloff, asking: Look Korsoniloff, have you ever had
a woman?

No answer.

Korsoniloff you skinny son of a bitch you never have
have you. You know what Korsoniloff you poor bastard I
just fucked the ass off an Armenian whore I did. Fucked
the ass right off her

To be precise, Korsoniloff, you're charged with disorderly

conduct. That is, under section 161 of the criminal code, sub-section 2, which reads 'everyone who wilfully disturbs or interrupts an assemblage of persons met for religious worship or for a moral, social, or benevolent purpose is guilty of an offence punishable on summary conviction.' Which means that you'll stand up in front of the magistrate and say guilty your honour and hand over the money.

But I'm not guilty.

Now look Korsoniloff, you told me this story right? You tried to mess up the wedding of your old girl friend or whatever. Now look, everyone understands that there might be hard feelings about something like that, maybe she should have sent you an invitation, but like I told you, you're guilty so you can just pay the goddam money and forget it.

Korsoniloff had never really liked Tonker. At one time it would have been possible for them to fight, predators, over the prey. But now it was not. Tonker was too fat.

Now look here. You're lucky you didn't get charged with assault. Mind you, you don't have to plead guilty. We could mess around, maybe countercharge the groom with goddam assault, fix the story a bit, take it to a judge and jury, put through a couple of appeals and maybe, who knows, we could get you off. It would take about a year and cost you, oh let's speak in round figures, fifteen hundred goddam dollars. On the other hand, the plaintiff might decide to sue you for the disruption of his wedding, assault and battery, and anything else his lawyer can think of. So look, at best it takes a year and costs you 15 goddam hundred. At worst it takes two years and costs 5 goddam thousand.

Tonker leaned back and opened his briefcase. Out came two jelly donuts—he offered one to Korsoniloff, who refused.

Now Korsoniloff, if you'll excuse me, I'll arrange bail and we can fuck off.

11

No thanks.

Tonker was still closing his briefcase and getting ready to go so Korsoniloff waited until he was standing up to say it again.

No thanks.

Now look Korsoniloff I don't goddam know what you're up to but if you're on one of your fucking idealistic kicks and want a fucking confrontation with the fucking judicial system a fucking disorderly conduct charge is a goddamfuckingstupid way to go about it.

Tonker looked at Korsoniloff who had lain down, exhausted. Alright, have it your way.   See you in court

Order. Order please. Everyone will rise. Yea yea yea this court is now in session. Will Raymond Cloves please step forward.

A short balding man rose and walked to the front of the courtroom.

What is your name?

Raymond Cloves.

Raymond Cloves you are charged with causing a disturbance by being drunk in a public place. How do you intend to plead?

Not guilty.

Speak louder.

Not guilty.

Will P. C. Warren please come forward and take the witness stand. Take the bible in your right hand. Do you swear to tell the truth?

Yes

What is your name in full?

Peter Armstrong Warren.

Now Officer Warren on the night of April the second

12

did you, at the intersection of Yonge and Wellesley, apprehend someone?

Yes.

Who was this man?

Him.

What was he doing?

He was pointing at passing cars and laughing and making rude remarks. I went up to him and I asked him what he thought he was doing.

What did he say?

Talking to the cars.

What happened then?

I asked him if he had been drinking and he said no. I then noticed he had a bulge in his jacket pocket and asked if he had something in his jacket pocket . . . You know . . .

What did he reply?

He said he did and pulled out a half-empty flask of whiskey. (Exhibit 1 your honour)

No further questions your honour.

Raymond Cloves step to the witness stand. Take this bible in your right hand. Do you swear to tell the truth?

Yes.

What is your full name?

Raymond Cloves.

Do you have anything to add to the testimony of the previous witness?

The bottle was full.

Speak up please.

The bottle in my jacket pocket was full and I hadn't been drinking.

Here is exhibit 1. Look at it carefully. Does it look like the bottle you had?

It's the same kind of a bottle but the one I had was full.

13

Have you been previously convicted for drunkenness?
Once.
When was that?
Three years ago.
In this court?
Yes.
Do you have anything further to say in your defence?
The bottle was full.
Do you have anything *further* to say in your defence?
No sir.
The court finds Raymond Cloves guilty of being drunk in a public place. One hundred dollars or thirty days. Two days to pay.
I don't get paid until next week.
Two days. Next case please.

Will André Korsoniloff step forward please. What is your name?
André Korsoniloff.
André Korsoniloff you are charged with wilfully disturbing an assembly of persons met for religious worship or for a moral, social or benevolent purpose. How do you intend to plead?
Not guilty.

III

So much for art. The preceding narrative prologue—such as it is—is merely the introductory façade through which I present myself. André Korsoniloff, Anglo-Russian by birth, teacher by trade, aspiring magician by nature. Aspiring yes, only aspiring. You will not find in me a virtuoso control of reality. Korsoniloff's only accomplishment is the complexity of his contradictions.

But I have dreams too. The lapse into literature serves to describe the moment in which Korsoniloff has finally outwitted himself; that is, acted himself into inactivity. And so I have moved one step forward towards the apocalypse which I await. The vision of destiny. The ultimate battle.

For you must know that my sedentary life is merely a mask beneath which my contrary selves struggle for supremacy. At one moment Korsoniloff, ever active, ever silent, seems finally vanquished. Body slack, relaxed, perceptions blurred, he lies defeated. I prepare to take over, ever-commenting narrator and officer of the nervous system. Finally I will have mastered Korsoniloff's impulses and made them my own. But at the very moment of triumph Korsoniloff re-appears.

Marie's image is evoked. Her face drains me of indepen-

15

dent existence and Korsoniloff once again begins pacing about, wondering where she is—while I re-assume my familiar stance. I comment. I point out his own foolishness. I demonstrate endlessly the futility of attachment. But to no avail. Korsoniloff, instinctually unable to accept less than everything, wallows in the pangs of deprivation.

How have I arrived in this position of utter stalemate? I can't promise to either bore or delight you with its history for I don't know myself. A word of caution. I warn you. Don't be taken in by the complex verbiage and the intricate patterns. For they are the curse of my aspirations. And it is my aspirations, rather than my birth or trade, that cause my constant misfortune. Or, to be precise, that have made me an opportunist by necessity. And that is exactly my position. My apartment is comfortable, not badly lit, and the table is adequate though without drawers. And my opportunity, now that I am rendered inactive in habitual realms, is to write the journal of my thirty-two years in the hope that it will teach me something.

Warnings. I could deliver pages and pages of advice to the reader and myself. But as I envision the endless tortured spirals another danger signal appears. For I am also (partially and dishonourably) a retired philosopher. Even the words cannot be trusted.

Indeed, I've often thought my misfortune may spring as much from my visual contradictions as those of my soul. Or, to be modern, my psyche. I stand about six feet two. A moderately high height accentuated by a thin body. But my head, unaccountably and not entirely unattractively, is almost completely round and covered with black hair. Which is somewhat by design as I wear a beard and luxuriant moustaches. In fact

But the disorderly-conduct charge. I must continually

16

reassure myself (or do I lament) that I am not a seducer of
young girls, a homosexual, nor even a drunk. Yet somehow,
I am now facing a morality charge.

A strange charge against a man such as myself. I think
of myself as essentially chaste. Not through virginity—not
being so decadent as to deny the senses—but, as it were, chaste
spiritually. Chastity is the virtue of the disciplined spirit, or,
as my contradictory elements advise me, the vice of the
perpetual child. I am then, a dilettante in nobility. At times
I meditate and am wonderfully transported. Otherwise I
make jokes, indulge in various Grand Projects, and play
Paralysis.

Inappropriate activity and compulsory rest. When I was
a student I was told to make my muse Apollo but the advice,
like all good advice, was completely impossible of realisation.

Hopes and visions. I wish to strip off all the scaffolding
and complexities, to emerge suddenly from behind the cape,
naked. But my disappearance leads to the same problems as
my attempts at mystery. Just as I relax my attachments out
pops Korsoniloff, ever-ready with exciting new plans and
passions, bouncing ahead until he trips.

Marie once said to me that she never knew what I was
thinking, that she never knew what I would say or do next.
Unknowingly she had touched upon one of my fondest aspirations. I wish to be nothing but behaviour.

One of the great bourgeois myths is that of
individual essence. That persons are more than what they do.
Korsoniloff with his overburdened personality, quirks and
eccentricities is not more but less than what he does. Personality, especially the kind that constitutes an eternal quali-
fication of actions, makes one less than what one does. That
is the reason so many

The desire to see the world as alternately triumph and

tragedy is the great illusion that makes history possible.

Writing about one's own childhood is never easy. Take the dock, for example.

Of course even children, though adults for their own purposes and self-suppression deny it, are burdened with consciousness. So the movement to pure behaviour is only symbolically a regression. One cannot remember what it was like to be without consciousness because to do so is self-contradictory.

My journal can be nothing but a series of connected curves spiralling towards a non-existent centre. I feel it is necessary to sink into the deepest of abysses to be finally purged of all these epiphenomenal mental symptoms. Or is this just another step in the complete paralysis of Korsoniloff? It is only our defences and rationalisations, the truths we keep from ourselves, that make thinking so deceptive.

We? Did I say we? Then it is time for another confession. I (he, Korsoniloff) intend this record for more than my own education, address you—please excuse the familiarity—in a sort of morality monologue.

Have you ever wondered, in the theatre, if the dividing line between players and audience is not somewhat arbitrary? Not only does the audience perform for itself—dressing for the occasion, marking each other's presence, enjoying its own laughter, applauding itself for its own tumultuous standing ovations—but it also performs for the actors. The actor knows the good audience from the bad one. He approaches it like a lover who knows his skill, attempting to evoke responses by the most subtle gesture—his power to move totally dependent upon the audience's willingness to be seduced into his game, to become the interplay of emotions on stage. The gestures of theatre must be larger than life—the actor is feeling not for himself, nor for the character he is portraying, but for the hundreds whose emotions he has tried to draw through himself. One would conclude that the actor, so dependent, ought to pay the audience for the pleasure of its response. And that is precisely why the audience pays the actors.

And why then does this admittedly arbitrary line exist? Purely for the pleasure that the various participants get from acting out their respective roles. But when the rationale is forgotten, when the roles become compulsory and people play only themselves, desperately maintaining their every vestige and detail of ego, then they experience only grief and frustration. They long for escape but act only to secure themselves in their own chains.

This for instance. If knowledge is the path to enlightenment, then I ought to be free of such encumbrances. But no, Korsoniloff is completely enslaved. Not only by his own passions and impulses—which even in themselves lead to enough problems—but also by myself—ever-chiding and reminding him that he drives himself deeper into his own circles.

What was I about to say? That we are all multiple role-players in any case and should learn to see the world as three-dimensional polygons of mirrors? I hope not; that is too commonplace. Besides, I have taken up residence in exile. My elaborations with the world are henceforth shifted. Korsoniloff adapts himself to the matrix and interstices of a vacuum to further his confrontation with himself. He takes on poses like a chameleon, and even fancies himself an interior decorator of sorts.

IV

The boy finally found a jersey on the bannister and so was clothed after all at the breakfast table. Pancakes, weekend pancakes with corn syrup, a pitcher of milk (you could tell it was powdered by the foam on top) a mottled orange and toast. André eats his food at a restrained rate, finally becomes absorbed peeling the orange trying to get the skin off in one piece and manages to forget he isn't alone.

I had wanted to move. Living with memories of Marie had been uncomfortable and now, after her marriage, unnecessary. So after Tonker paid my bail I did. When I told Smythe—my colleague and landlord—I was leaving he smiled his embarrassed smile and mumbled something about not minding since his wife had wanted extra space anyway.

Your honour I have two witnesses to call.
Proceed.
They are not able to be present. They are on their honeymoon.
What are their names?
Harold Melten and his wife Mrs. Marie Melten.

20

When will they be back?
In three weeks your honour. A remand has been requested.
Granted.

Tonker, irresistibly efficient, posted bond after my
appearance in court. The trial was set for June 23rd. Meanwhile
Korsoniloff is in a pseudo-cell, this basement apartment, with
a landlady who is a collection of innuendoes and a dehumidifier.

There is a living-room, a kitchen and a small bedroom
off the kitchen. The furnishings, aside from the solid table
and a stuffed armchair, consist almost solely of narrow single
beds and 1930 Eaton's-catalogue dressers. There is a dresser
in the bedroom for clothes. Two dressers in the livingroom
to fill up the corners and a dresser in the kitchen for plates,
food, and the innumerable white doilies that were on the
other dressers.

Before Marie, on days when Korsoniloff felt lonely, he
would wander around, looking in bookstores and having coffee
in restaurants, hoping that something would happen. Some
days there are so many people wandering about, encased in
their separateness, that you almost wonder why they don't
speak to each other. Korsoniloff would stop in a bookstore,
scanning titles and watching out of the corner of his eye
for a gesture, the subtlest movement that could be construed
as an invitation. Then finally, having given the world its
chance, he would close off his senses and leave the store.

Marie, though, disdaining such furtiveness, had just called
him up and asked him to meet her for a drink. Oh yes—
their names were known to each other. A few encounters in
the university corridors, a seminar or two which they had
both attended. Names and faces.

Do you know, she had said, do you know that I don't
do this as a habit?

No, he thought, I bet you don't. Looking at her rounded face and eyes, you look innocent enough to smile in that certain way in front of the mirror every morning.

I've wanted to talk to you for a long time, she said, and everyone said you drank a lot so I thought this would be the best way. He watched her mouth move; the teeth and lips were colour-sharp. He wanted to kiss her and know that she would kiss him. But the words.

Did you, he said, that's very nice.

Parenthetically, at this point, I note that Korsoniloff was well warned. Even while they played the words of the encounter I wondered about the grade-B come-on.

I wanted us to talk of course.

Of course. You meet these people every day. They send you postcards in the mail and laugh at all the wrong times.

After another silence Marie suggested that we go for a walk so we went outside and strolled about; she talked small-talk about herself and just as I was thinking again about how the evening had started she informed me that we were outside her door and said goodnight. So I was left standing there, half wanting more (although more of what wasn't clear) and half in a panic trying to figure out what was happening.

If there's anything that hooked me right then it was the panic. It made me realize how bored I had been. What was there to be afraid of? The possibility of finding out fascinated me. But after a few days the incident faded. I thought of phoning her but there didn't seem to be any point. Korsoniloff re-immersed himself in alternating bouts of busyness and strung-out aloneness.

About two weeks after that I was sitting at home reading a few term papers, when Marie appeared at the door.

22

Hi, she said. I just thought I'd drop by. So she came in
and we had coffee and told each other about all the nothing
things we were doing. Again she left abruptly, this time
precipitating less a panic than a definite feeling of uncom-
fortableness. But this time, instead of being fascinated by it,
I attributed it to Korsoniloff's only sporadically satisfied lust
(the fall seems to be his main mating season and he was
having a bad year in that respect) and let it go.

After that the visits came more frequently. Every
three or four days she would appear; a kind of familiarity
developed. It was as if we had once been lovers and now
had some symbiotic need for each other that could be gratified
by blank conversations and mild affirmations of friendship.
I even began stopping at her place occasionally. We would
sit in the living-room of the apartment she shared with two
other graduate students and listen to her records.

It was the times I visited her that the tension of our
first meeting was hinted at. We would sit in the dark listening
to records (her room-mates seemed to have sleeping sickness)
not talking, till finally she would suggest we go into the
kitchen and have some coffee. This I took as a signal for my
imminent departure and after finishing the coffee (taken
with milk so it would be finished quickly) I would say goodbye. Sometimes I wondered if I surprised her as much by
leaving as she had once surprised me, but by this time I
had come to take her innocence so much for granted that any
sexual contact was out of the question.

One night, remembering how her lips had looked to me
when we first met, and seeing them that way again, I leaned
over and kissed her. The illusion of relaxation vanished and
Korsoniloff started to sink into her sensuousness.

No, she said, you're not sincere.

I was just going to demonstrate my sincerity when one of

her room-mates, resurrected into a wrap-around purple quilt, walked in. I left feeling distinctly uneasy, foregoing the usual coffee

(can you remember)

The boy goes outside after breakfast. Stands on the lawn and then walks down towards the spring creek. He finds himself under his tree and climbs up to where he sits. This is his tree. Also his sanctuary; it is understood that when he is in the tree he cannot be disturbed. In the winter it is claimed by ice and snow though still he sometimes climbs it. But in the spring it becomes completely his; André would go out and sit in it for hours looking at the spring snow and the patches of ground. The creek is almost dry now but his fantasy is of a rushing river, as big as the Ottawa, sweeping under him. One day he'll build a raft and go with the river to the St. Lawrence, to the sea. Sitting in the tree, watching all the separate leaves go through their wind-patterns, it is hours since he was in bed thinking and staring

V

Korsoniloff's schedule had been punctured. The original suspicion of an unknown element confirmed itself. He would wait for a knock at the door. Jump when the telephone rang hoping it was Marie. But somehow he was too paralysed to be able to go see her. The incident went round and round. Should I have stayed and outwaited the purple Lazarus? Should I apologise?—but there's nothing to apologise for. Should I forget the whole thing and let us, resume the usual mode of interaction? Which was what I thought Marie to be doing. Obviously the friendship was important to her, but it had to be

Therefore, when Marie called three days later, Korsoniloff was decidedly restrained—he left late and arrived just before midnight.

The child and the man. They exist, at best, in uneasy truce. Neither totally approving of the other but bound by the resemblance. The dreams fulfilled turn out to be empty, those forgotten or unrealised have drifted irrevocably by. Irrevocable. Time always appears irrevocable. But I am cast into these fragments of the past so wholly. No one can ever entirely succeed in distancing themselves from their own experience. A

André sitting in the tree, waiting for the creek to grow, caught a glimpse of silver. Watched it. Came down and went over. A quarter; put it in his pocket and forgot it. An hour later came to a stand.

Want to buy some cherries André? Eat them right out of the basket or cool them. Eat them cold they're best cold.

Behaviour and consciousness. André Korsoniloff alternates between these two reliable categories. But are they? Is not activity a contemplative form, and introspection a mode of action? The officer of the watch records his own log. One of my duties is to point out my own traps so that you will not fall into them. And, of course, vice versa.

Oh, I'm glad you came. I was afraid you were angry. She followed him into the living room turning down the lights as she always did.

No, not at all. We sat on the couch and Marie put on some records—the usual light jazz and blues, fresh from a coffee-house Muzak supplier. It was hard to imagine how we had sat there so relaxed before. We didn't talk much, just a few phrases about cigarettes and weather. We smoked. We had a cup of coffee. After about an hour Marie turned over the records. The few seconds of silence were painful and we sat up straight until the arm came down to the first record. Then we leaned back, the space between us filled with sound. We sat and smoked. Marie offered more coffee and I said no thanks. The hour passed and the records were turned.

The whole time I was, in a dozing way, obsessed with the idea of kissing her again—but it seemed like too much to be bothered with. Without worrying about it I sank deeper and deeper into paralysis. It was getting cold. The records were ready to be turned again. When she stood up I lay full length on the couch, sure that it would precipitate something.

You must be tired, she said. Why don't I pull the couch out into a bed. Why not? I thought. I live all of four blocks away. Which she knows. She knows I know. I know she knows. Then we both know what's happening. It was funny that we could both know what was happening and still have it not happen. I sat on the couch-bed. It sagged. She went over to a cupboard and got a quilt, brought it to me.

Here, she said, starting to put it over me, this will be warm. You can't sit on the edge of a couch-bed and have a quilt put over you, so I lay down. We both know what's happening, I thought, I wish it would hurry up and happen. I was going to embrace her when she sat down on the edge of the bed. The whole thing was getting too protracted.

She leaned over me, smiling—don't be afraid to fall asleep. Then she went over to an adjacent armchair and sat down.

Marie, I said.

Yes.

Goodnight.

I had intended to say something more to the point but 'goodnight' had popped out so I let it stay there. It was too much. Just too much. After a while I must have dozed because light was showing through the curtains when I next looked up. I became aware of her standing at the door.

Goodnight, she said turning. I hoped she hadn't waited till I woke up to say it.

André sitting on the rail, numb, the words buzzing through him, André I hope you'll love Bess, I do. (He's trembling you died too young. I'm probably doing the wrong thing but if I didn't that would be wrong too you died too young can Bess bring you back into the world you're too

27

young to have memories André say something pleasesay) yes
speak Father is this really her is it really is it

Hi Mrs. Kilber.

Korsoniloff don't you ever relax?
Fuck you Tonker.

André came up to the stand, remembered the quarter.
Sure I'd like to. Tell me which is the best basket. Look what
I found. They examined the quarter and then the cherries. Hey
Mrs. Kilber, how could you make cherries cold if you didn't
have a refrigerator?
Walking back to the house, ducking around the side and
then put the basket up in the tree. Back to the house. No one
in the kitchen. A bowl and some cold water.
One for me, one for you, counted André, putting
cherries alternately in his mouth and the bowl. Cheating
only at the end when he took the last three and
Well, said Mikhail, pushing out from the table, how
about something cold for dessert? Bess started to get up.
No, let me, just a minute. André ran out of the house
down to his tree and the bowl in the shade. Ate a cherry. It
was good. Cold. Raced back to the house. Stopped outside
the door to have another. Looked at it. It was split. They
had all split. Opened the door.

Come here. She came over and sat beside me. It was so
tenuous; she was so innocent. I kissed her and pulled her
down beside me. I kept kissing her and started stroking her
more or less inert back. Then, hesitantly, she began kissing
me in a way that struck me as a weird combination of sen-
suous and chaste. So innocent, I was thinking, and her hand

28

slid down my shirt and under my pants.

Finally I was about to enter her. Everything about her had become luxuriantly sexual. Korsoniloff was supreme in his intensity. As he entered her an alarm clock in the next room went off. We paused. She blushed. I realised I wasn't the first but that had begun to dawn on me some time previous. I was supporting myself on my elbows and my shoulders were beginning to ache. The sky was changing colours. I came inside her, Marie's eyes and mine locked, and Korsoniloff took the ascendant.

What can I say to excuse or explain? Analytic comments? I have none. That we should have lived happily ever after? We didn't, clearly. Though at times I wanted it. One can never really deal simultaneously with beginnings and middles. The beginning antedates the middle and the middle is drawn from what antedated the beginning. In any case beginnings are utopian always, middles never.

Was I disillusioned when I discovered Marie's innocence was not literal?

No, I was not.

Did I realise then that she was not innocent in any specifiable sense and dismiss the concept as my own mental construct?

No, I did not.

If I wished to release her from inexperience did she want to refresh my decadence?

I hoped so.

No one should ever play saviour for anyone else. Not because it doesn't work, but because there's nothing to gain. If the role fails the saviour is frustrated. If it succeeds, worse—disaster. The saviour is robbed of his partner in the game.

Do I say this out of the profound conviction of my

experience with Marie?

Or did I realise it beforehand?

No and yes.

Then there was more insight than wisdom?

Unfortunately.

My fear of Marie dissolved. I became the guardian of her emergent sexuality. I took upon myself the mission of a transcendental reconciliation. Whereas I was bored with myself she was, to herself, undiscovered.

Which is not to say that I entered into the relation because of a psychological match. No indeed. I went along with it conceding a certain interest but Korsoniloff, as I admitted above, Korsoniloff had ascended.

VI

Since I moved I've gone into my office twice at night to deal with correspondence—otherwise have stayed away from the university. How solitary I've become was made apparent last night.

I went upstairs to see the landlady; something had gone wrong with the basement plumbing. She was sitting in the kitchen talking to one of the tenants, a man, fiftyish, introduced to me as Mr Hartford. Mr Hartford, or Clarence as he became shortly, had brought down a steak for Mrs Fairlane and invited me to join them. I contributed two bottles of good wine I had been saving and we drank them with the meal. It seemed a long time since I had eaten with people. Whether it was that or just the influence of the wine I found Patsy more and more enjoyable as the evening progressed. Perhaps with Marie I had become addicted to an element of reserve, an inappropriate modesty. In Patsy there is none of this, she seems directly herself. She isn't a big woman, but she moves and talks with the solid assurance associated with size. The 'Mrs' it turned out during the second bottle of wine is fictitious. She assumed it several years ago, when she took the house, to discourage male tenants.

During the meal she constantly paid small attentions to

both myself and Clarence who, anti-numinally, is extremely stocky and extremely bald. But dialectically affirmed by his apprenticeship in chartered accountancy. Our fraternal drunkenness increased. Patsy focussed in on Clarence. As I left they were deciding to throw rubber darts at the television set.

I came back downstairs, slightly dizzy, just before midnight. Lay down, put on some music—surfeited with food, wine, and being with people. Just being around others requires a great amount of nervous energy. Was on the verge of going to sleep when the phone rang.

Hello Korsoniloff, Alex here. Now look here Korsoniloff it's time you got up and out. I'm at a party and I've sent a cab over to your place; see you in a few minutes.

I hadn't had time to say a word. He couldn't even have been sure it was me who had answered. Before I had time to start to figure out what to do, Patsy, looking a bit worse for wear, came knocking at my door and told me there was a cab out front for me.

It was in one of the new apartment buildings near Bay Street. The driver, obviously on instruction, took me up to the suite. He shrugged off my attempt to pay him and opened the door. There were too many people to bother looking around. Here, someone said, handing me a glass. I drank it. Tonker came over, slapped me on the back and disappeared.

I looked for the door but had already been pushed into the centre of the room. Someone was talking about antique clocks. It appeared that the host had a collection of them in some room. Thinking it might be less crowded, I went looking for it. Down a hall. First door, bathroom. Second door, bedroom. Third door. Fourth door. Four people.

Students, they looked like. Sit down, one said. Thanks. Like the clocks? said another. Sure, I said, looking around for them. There was a pot of tea and some cups on the desk. Want

some? the girl asked. Sure thanks, feel a bit dizzy. I poured
myself some and drank the cup in one gulp. It had an almost
incense-like aroma. Poured another one. You like the tea?
one young man asked. He had a funny smile and his eyes
seemed extra-sharply focussed. Yes, I said, yes.

We sat silent for a few minutes. Feeling better now? the
girl asked. Sure, feel fine. Someone said something about the
party and they got up to leave. Stay if you want, the girl said,
I'll be back later.

There were paper and pens on the desk beside the tea.
Decided to write about this evening for my journal. How would
the clocks sound if they were all ticking? Won't tick even if I
listen. Like writing on this desk green blotter

No one here. Feel shaky. What's happening? Don't want
to go back to the party. If I do   Tonker

Marie. your name looks strange.
Marie
Bess
Anna
Mikhail
André

Last night I dreamt about a cat. Dark orange and black fur.
Bushy tail. Walked-leapt everywhere. Cat on the window sill.
Black around the window but green sill. Looked out to street
concrete, two sidewalks, trees. Cat and I looked at the trees. No.
Too far. Hydro pole. Man on the hydro pole watching me and
the cat. Takes out a rifle and sights along it. Am staring into
the pool of the muzzle. He shoots. I jump but it hits the cat.
Bleeding it goes around room apparently unaffected. Follow
it, am in pain, both of us hopping about the room

No one here. Listen the clocks starting tick. Grandfather's

33

polished walnut in the hall. Mikhail said he had the hour bells
taken out, it woke them in the night.

ANDRE KORSONILOFF STEP FORWARD TO THE STAND
YES YOUR HONOUR
YOU STAND ACCUSED OF MATRICIDE AND FORNICATION
YES YOUR HONOUR
HOW DO YOU INTEND TO PLEAD?
GUILTY YOUR HONOUR.
DON'T YOU HAVE A CLEAN SHIRT KORSONILOFF?
I'LL GET ONE RIGHT AWAY YOUR HONOUR.
YOU CAN'T BE HANGED WITHOUT A CLEAN SHIRT KOR-
SONILOFF
HANGMAN AT THE SCAFFOLD WEARS RED POLKA-DOT
KERCHIEF,   CONSOLES THE WEEPING JURY WHO
BREAKAWAY
PRAY FOR DEAD MAN'S SOUL AND
MARCH AROUND HIS EMPTY GRAVE
ANDRE KORSONILOFF DO YOU HAVE ANYTHING TO SAY
BEFORE
NO YOUR HONOUR SIR
DO YOU RECOGNIZE THIS PICTURE
YES
WHO IS IT KORSONILOFF
MY MOTHER SIR
WHY DID YOU DO IT
I DIDN'T DO IT SIR IT WASN'T I IT WAS KORSONILOFF WHO
DID IT
AND WHO ARE YOU THEN?
WHY ME SIR
SORRY KORSONILOFF THAT WON'T DO AT ALL. I'M AFRAID
WE'LL HAVE TO

34

WAIT A MINUTE STOP WAIT A MINUTE STOP
WHAT'S THE MATTER KORSONILOFF?
IT'S NOT ME IT'S HIM. THERE HE IS STANDING THERE
THAT'S WHO IT   IS
LOOK AT HIM HE DID IT
OFF WITH HIS HEAD OFF WITH HIS HEAD

oh god I'm absolutely dead nothing absolutely nothing
except my voice saying nothing except my voice saying except
my voice   quiet be absolutely quiet   why can't I stop thinking
thoughts clutter up the vacuum   the vacuum   the vacuum

GOODMORNING ladies and gentlemen   we bring you the
eight o'clock news. To-day, at six o'clock in the morning, at
the Don Jail, André Korsoniloff was beheaded as a consequence
of his conviction for matricide and fornication. Witnesses say
that although he had to be told to change his shirt he behaved
bravely and made minimal fuss. Let us all join in prayer for
his soul wherever it may be

ANDRE

hello there all you wonderful people out there   we bring
you to-day your favourite program of baltic-russo folk-dancing
and singing and we have here to-day, as our special guest,
calvin coolidge. calvin, tell me, how are you to-day

fine thank you, just fine. but before proceeding with my
famous balto-russian snake song i'd like to say a few words on
behalf of our sponsor, america deodorant. now folks, as you
know, odour offends. i don't mean to say that any of you out
there are actually smelly, but
OH COME ALL YE FAITHFUL

35

you know that when the weather gets
JOYFUL AND TRIUMPHANT
hot is the time you have to be
OH COME YE O COME YE
especially careful   why just the other day i
BE-Ethle-HEM
was saying to my wife
JESUS LOVES ME
GODDAMIT CLARA YOU STIN
YES I KNOW
ky
TANK   THANK   YOU THANK YOU THANKYOUONEANDALL

I broke the plaster icon but it was glued up and good as
new except for the seams where you could see it had been
glued up where I broke it
    jesusfuckingchristaintthissomething
    PROCEED TO THE BEATITUDES
    excuse me mr announcer it's kind of you to come along
but i think i'll just have to leave   goodbye

    whoopy doo.

    and said goodbye to time.
    The girl came back. Where are you, she asked.
    Pardon?
    Where are you.
    Oh me. Right here fine thank you why don't you sit down
    My name's gail
    Gail. What a nice name. How nice of Tonker to lead me
to you. Well, if you'll excuse me gail.

VII

When I woke up Gail was sitting across from me, drinking coffee and reading. Hi, I said, when is it? She consulted her watch; it was noon. We went into the kitchen—there were a few people asleep on the living-room floor and couch but no sign of Tonker.

Have you lived here long? I asked as she began scrambling some eggs.

A few months.

What do you do?

Get up in the mornings, see people, read the papers, have parties.

Your husband?

I'm not married. Do you like salt and pepper?

I ate the eggs and then got up to go.

Stay if you like, we could watch television or something.

Thanks, I'd better be off.

I'm not sure why I left—maybe it seemed like an offer to start in at the beginning of something that had already ended. When I got home there was a letter waiting for me with Hotel Hilton emblazoned on the outside.

Dear André,

Harold and I talked about you for a long time yesterday. He, as much as I, regrets the unfortunate episode at our wedding. We decided I should write you, not only to tell you that we bear no ill feelings towards you but also so that I might have a chance to set the record straight.

Although, in a way, I loved you, and I'm sure that you loved me, I think I must have been pretty confused when I entered our relationship. Although I'm grateful for it—I've never regretted having known you and I realize it must have helped us both to become more mature, wiser, persons— neither have I regretted my decision to stop seeing you, painful and difficult though it was at the time.

Harold, and I hope you two can meet under less strained circumstances some time, is, for whatever reason, the kind of man I need to make me happy. I love him, feel secure with him, and know that things have worked out for the best for me.

I've thought about you a lot, André, since we last saw each other. I always wondered if you really knew me, or for that matter, if I really knew you. We're so different you and I; it's amazing we could have got along even the way we did. When I think about you, I always wonder if you, a person of such potential, are really fulfilling yourself.

I know you have a good job and get along well with the students but, André, that's not what I mean. I wonder if, perhaps,—I hope you don't mind me saying this—your view of the world isn't distorted towards the unhappy and the pessimistic. God knows, André, there's enough to be unhappy about in this world, but sometimes I think you see that too exclusively of the happiness.

Have you ever thought of taking psycho-therapy André? I know that you're not crazy or insane, but perhaps it could help you see yourself with a little more perspective, accept

38

*yourself more. You once told me that you wished you could
be more relaxed; maybe this would help.*

*Harold, as you may know, is a psychologist. Although he
does mostly experimental work at the laboratory, he did say
he could probably recommend someone for you. Well, André,
I don't mean to intrude into your personal life; I hope you'll
think about this.*

*Perhaps you can come over to dinner sometime after we
get back to Toronto,*

Regards,
(Mrs) Marie Melten

After Marie and I made love that first time we lay on the
couch looking out at the morning. It was easy to be there, to
look out the window and at each other. To let our bodies
settle into each other, comfortable and tired. But the sounds
of the adjacent room-mate getting up threatened to disturb
that and I decided to go while everything was still intact.

I remember, leaving, that there seemed to be some question
of whether what had happened was a conclusion or a beginning,
but I felt so good, Korsoniloff having achieved his total victory,
that the question was made irrelevant. I walked up the street,
smiling and nodding to my fellow early-risers, watching the
smoke puff into the blue-grey sky and feeling altogether at
peace. When I got home I climbed into bed, felt again the
softness of her flesh, and fell into a deep sleep.

When I woke up it was noon. I had to give a class at one
so I walked, half-ran, down to the university. After the class I
had to see some students about papers, that night there was a
seminar, so all in all it was two days before I had time to sit
down leisurely and think about the affair with Marie. It was
evening; I had come home after attending (though before then
I rarely did) one of the endless department meetings held to

discuss strategies to outwit the administration. Smythe, interminably concerned, had invited me downstairs for a drink and I had begged off saying that I wanted to sleep for a while. Been staying up late, he said with his usual dry touch and then burst into a fit of coughing and laughing. The wife says she saw you coming home at eight the other morning. Never seen you awake so early, she said. Well, take it easy. He broke into another fit.

Once upstairs I began to feel restless and started wondering whether Marie would welcome a call from me. Often as not she would have called or come over in the time since I had last seen her and I found myself trying to decide whether to attach significance to the fact that she hadn't.

Poor Korsoniloff. Once hooked always finds the game reversed. Thought about that for a while, lectured myself on the rewards of mastering the senses, then gave up and phoned Marie.

Hello, I said, just thought I'd see how you've been.

Fine. There was a silence.

Would you like to go out for a drink or something later?

I felt foolish asking that—why wasn't I confident? Had not Korsoniloff established the crucial rapport? Finally she made it easy . . . suggested I come down to her place later and listen to some music.

If she had really been hesitant when I called she wasn't when I arrived. Showing me that the living-room door had a lock on it she locked it, put on some records, turned out the lights, and pulled out the couch. We made love, for hours it seemed, and fell asleep together on the couch. When the alarm went off the next morning we both woke up, looked at each other and grinned, and fell back to sleep. When I woke up again, a couple of hours later, I got dressed, kissed her, and left.

That night she came up to my place and we stayed there. For weeks we spent almost every night together. We would meet late, just before midnight—later if either of us had been busy—make love half the night, and then fall asleep. I came to know her by candle-light and streetlights through the windows. What we were doing seemed so forbidden to her that she was only really comfortable making love at night. The few times we met in the afternoon seemed somehow strained and abbreviated.

But at night our time stretched out endlessly. Though she seemed slim, almost spare, dressed, her flesh was luxuriously soft. Each time we started to make love I felt I was sinking into a world of infinite sensuality; I felt completely at home, like a child in an utterly benevolent land.

Korsoniloff was so dominant that he seemed for once rid of dual consciousness. It was the perfect holiday.

But after a few weeks the nights began to take their toll. When we dream, but never act, we have the pleasures of our fantasies without the consequences. But when, by chance or design, our lives become such that there exists the opportunity to act out the wishes that have been previously only half-known, strange things begin to happen.

For some reason, perhaps some sense of power kindled with Marie, I had started attending the department meetings I had previously so assiduously avoided. One Wednesday, they were regularly on Wednesdays for two hours with a twenty-minute break for small jam sandwiches and coffee, the problem of student evaluation came up.

I suggested, or was it Korsoniloff—in such situations I lose all control and speak as if possessed, as surprised as anyone at what comes out—that all examinations and essays be dropped and that henceforth students be permitted, forced if necessary, to devise their own means, if any, of testing and evaluation.

By the time I had finished, horrified as all the rest, I realised that Korsoniloff, in a ruthlessly efficient manoeuvre, had succeeded in ostracising my intellectual self. How could I say I didn't really mean it, it was just a joke played on me by a witless daemon? I, who despite my youthful feelings of a few years ago had played the intellectual conservative to the point where I had disdained to converse about philosophy with my own colleagues.

There was a brief silence, then with a 'Hm that's very interesting indeed' the meeting proceeded as if nothing had happened. Afterwards I walked home with Smythe. Just before we went in he said 'You're a cold fish Korsoniloff, I wouldn't have thought you would give a damn about anything'.

Me cold? With my secret lusts and satanic nights. Me, my career turned upside down by Korsoniloff—who is nothing but a bundle of supercharged impulses? Cold?

VIII

It was a terrifying thought. In fact, as I paced about my apartment I realized that I had never wondered how, outside of my physical characteristics, I appeared to other people. Was I warm or cold, funny or boring? Was my small-talk small enough or was it filled with intellectual pretentiousness? Did I face the world as Korsoniloff or did the world see the part of me that observed him? Why would Smythe come out with a statement like that?

I poured myself a drink. This whole matter was ridiculous, I had no doubt about that. Marie had seen me, both professionally and intimately. I decided to ask her and called her up immediately.

Marie, am I a cold fish?
What's the matter?
No, tell me, do I strike you as cold?
Her answers were entirely unsatisfactory. She had, at first, found me unemotional; but then, getting to know me, she had seen the opposite. But yes, some people might find me cold, I didn't exactly strike a first-impression of heartiness. We arranged to meet later and then rang off. I sat quiet for a

moment, then on sudden inspiration got a sheet of paper and began writing down names—names of students, names of friends, names of acquaintances. Beside each of their names I would write either warm or cold. But then, after all, what was meant by those terms? So and so is known to be good-hearted. A friendly smile and a greeting for all. But when you really need him where is he? Still smiling and saying hello, how are you. On the other hand someone else is thought to be mean. Never a kind word for anything or anyone. But when there is difficulty the old Scrooge is right there, willing to help out any way he can. It seemed, as I ran down the list, that the more I thought about it the less I was able to assign anyone their quality.

But of course. How that suited my own vested interests. Was not Korsoniloff constantly masqueraded as polite, intellectual and ascetic? Was he not always tactfully withdrawn after outbursts like that of this afternoon?

It became clearer and clearer. What I was offended by was not the particular of being cold—it was the idea of being anything at all. Always obeying, I had thought, the dictum of philosophy I had indulged and encouraged endless introspection. But in fact the reality was, not only did I not know myself but I had no intention whatsoever of self-knowledge. In fact I found the goal both impossible and undesirable.

Excuse me if I dwell upon that evening, or retrace too laboriousl the details of my labyrinth. But how else can it be understood why, at that moment, I decided that my inner forces had been misaligned, a decision that I have, of course, fulfilled and reversed with my intercession at Marie's wedding.

In any case, confronted with my own opacity, I realised that the darkness was a result of my persistent efforts to hide and subdue Korsoniloff. Who, despite the energy directed at his destruction, was presently prevailing in all areas. Was not this tenacity proof in itself of his being the essential me? Instead of trying to smother him, me, I should give in and let events proceed untramelled. Give up my bland exterior and become completely random.

Does one really decide what to be or just rationalise after the fact? No matter, for whichever one takes to be true it remains that thanks to Smythe's comment the change which I regarded as the most momentous of my adult life was catalysed.

What does one do after presiding over one's own rebirth? Nothing in particular. Of course. Await events. If one configuration changes surely the rest will follow. Having decided that I was, indeed, Korsoniloff, I confidently expected that I could continue my usual pursuits with the assurance that the transformation would eventually make itself evident.

I must admit that when I informed Marie of the apocalypse she didn't take it too seriously. She viewed it, I suppose, as an indication of my nervous condition—I always expected her, though she never did, to say that there was nothing that couldn't be remedied by a good mixture of prayer and calisthenics. However, although she paid little attention to my announcement at the time, the matter became crucial to our relationship. Nemesis, one might say; for Korsoniloff—set free by our relationship—also destroyed it.

Ramblings. Am I trying to escape the letter which has sat—apparition-like and not particularly welcome—on my desk for the last day? I don't know what to think or do about it. Called Tonker and asked if Melten was in a position to drop charges; no. He told me that Gail had gotten my address and phone number from him and to expect to see her shortly.

That night with the clocks. Seemed as if neither Korsoniloff nor his watchdog held the key to anything but their own patterns.

45

After I left Gail

Excuse me

André won't fight, André won't fight

I heard them chanting in a circle around him in the school-
yard. He was lying on his face in the dust and the grass. Each
blade set into a mound. Terry on top of him twisting his
arm into his back.
Give up Korsoniloff?
My position in this matter is, of course, unchanged so I
have no choice except
He wanted to. No he didn't. In a way it was so totally
peaceful, a relief, to be finally in the middle of it, to
Well I must say I'm surprised at your stubbornness; you
might try to understand our point of view
No
André hit him André. Roll over hit him. Let him have it
Terry
Of course
You understand, Korsoniloff, that even if you don't
receive tenure
He got a foot around the back of Terry's ankle then pushed
It will come up again next year with, I hope, more fa-
vourable results. I'm sure you'll be able to modify
Around. His left elbow must have snapped back because
Terry was winded now he sat on top
Get him get him back
If you ever say that again I'll
Motherfucker
Oh André hit him. Hit him again   hit
Pardon?

46

Okay Korsoniloff
Want to quit fighting
Sure
Okay let's get up
  Why'd you let him off so easy   you should have hit
him again you

IX

It has been several days, a week in fact, since I last wrote anything. The hiatus, a forced vacation at best, is not entirely due to the fact that I have been otherwise occupied. In a way I wish it were. The real reason

Control is the key. I seem to need to retain control over what I am writing. One would think that should be very easy. After all, I don't have to write anything I don't want to. But then, the same could apply to anything. I don't have to say or do anything I don't want to either.

I should admit to having a very neat mind. It is compartmentalised nicely into the rational and the irrational. I lead my life; Korsoniloff leads his. From time to time there is a shift in the balance of forces; the 'I', as it were, switches to the new prevailing direction. This is regarded as a most satisfactory arrangement. However on occasion, as if to demonstrate that all categories are indeed illusory if carried beyond a certain point, the contiguous nature, the line of contiguity of the compartments to be precise, comes into the foreground and unline-like proceeds to spread itself and obscure all else.

Although theoretically this should be a welcome, a euphoric experience—integration and liberation—it is in fact nothing of the sort. Conversely it brings forth, expands beyond their usual 1-dimensional domain, certain conflicts with which, to be candid, I am completely unable to deal. My mind becomes a maze of questions, unhappily unrhetorical, and answers, completely unacceptable, which run themselves in circles until from exhaustion or subconscious volition they quiet themselves and fade back to their proper recesses. Nor am I solely, when they finally do recede, relieved; I always feel distinctly uneasy and wish that I might resolve whatever it is that is so provoked.

If the present periodic outburst suggests that I have found a way through my dilemma then I should make it clear that I haven't. I feel like the proverbial cartoonist who has put his hero in a position so impossible of solution that, in order to continue his strip and his income, he must resort to piling detail upon detail in the hope that finally, as the situation becomes infinitely intricate, everyone will have forgotten how it all began and he can sneak his hero out the side door without anyone noticing.

Being my own protagonist, of course, adds a certain inapplicability to the analogy. For if, in fact, I do manage to sidestep the whole matter it is only at the cost of going incommunicado with myself. Nonetheless we do sometimes resort to that measure.

A few hours after I spoke to Tonker Gail did, as predicted, make an appearance. Though I seldom notice such things she immediately struck me as smartly dressed. At her apartment she had seemed somehow out of place amidst her own possessions—as if she were slightly spoiled. Now she appeared a very elegant young woman who knew what she wanted. Which, as I didn't, made me suspicious.

She came in, announced by Patsy, and sat down. Pulling out a cigarette from a leather cigarette case and lighting it with (of course) an alligator skin lighter, she asked for a drink. I

brought her a scotch and played with the ice in mine, pushing
it down and watching it bounce up while she sipped and
talked about the trouble she was having with her MG. She
finished her cigarette, put it out in the green and white ceramic
angel with a hole in the navel that Patsy provided for such
occasions, and announced that the purpose of her visit was to
induce me to come out to dinner with her if I wasn't already
busy.

We went to a steak-house, she had been wanting a steak
for days, and dined well. There was a minimum of polite
interaction. Afterwards, without asking me what I wanted to
do, she drove us back to her apartment. When we were finally
settled in, opposite each other in black leather armchairs that
swivelled and rocked in every direction, she with a cigarette
lit with her alligator skin lighter and myself likewise, I decided

What's going on?
What do you mean?
The party, the tea, Tonker, the dinner?
Yes.
Don't they seem a bit strange to you?
No. Do they to you?
Not to ask any questions.
André?

Clarence came down the next night primed for serious
discussion. Persons who decide late in life to become intellec-
tuals seem without fail to have two characteristics with regard
to their new knowledge. The first, which generally elicits a
negative response from professionals, is an unselective stubbornness about anything that is written down

You seem tense

The second, which usually goes unnoticed, is an almost absolute honesty. In the course of pursuing his second career Clarence had discovered psychology and Freud. He was currently reading Freud cover to cover (the collected works) and had run into a footnote which included a phrase in German—he thought perhaps, being a professor

My expansions of contiguity, while always unwilled, are generally preceded by a recognisable rumbling in the back of my mind,—making me of course, wary of extended discussions of psychology

Gail did indeed look nervous, curled into her armchair, smoking steadily. I began to wonder again

As for himself, Clarence said a second time, he couldn't see any great significance in his dream life. He did, naturally, remember the odd dream, even some he wouldn't want to talk about, but they didn't tell him anything he didn't know

Before she replied to my question she made a movement as if to get up and then decided not to. No particular reason, she said, I was just feeling lonely and wanted to go out to dinner with someone. I felt silly for asking and tried to make up for it. She brought out some hidden paternal protectiveness in me, though she only seemed child-like at her own place. Before leaving I said she should come over again and self-assuredly, as though the kink in the conversation hadn't happened, she saw me to the door and held my arm briefly but not in promise, as I left.

So when she came over one afternoon, two or three days later, I wasn't surprised to see her and was glad to accompany her on a drive in the country. We found a restaurant on a dirt road and had sandwiches, then went back to Toronto and Gail's apartment.

Clarence had concluded, the day before, that although he really couldn't take the dream theory seriously, he should write his dreams down in the morning just to see what happened. Sure enough, the next morning he woke up with an elaborate dream which, he informed me, he couldn't show me just yet but it took up four pages and he was going to keep doing it. I was jealous; I can't remember any four page dreams, and hoped I could see his sometimes.

She asked me if I wanted some tea and after sitting on the couch I would wonder at each moment if the previous had occurred or was just dreamed. I would ask Gail and then sink deeper wondering if the whole checking process had occurred or was just
She said she had to ask me one question first though I might find it strange it was important to her. Sure, I said, curious what it might be
Each movement was so infinitely protracted that it was impossible to know how long we had
No, I said, it doesn't matter if you love me, why do you ask?

X

Strangely, Korsoniloff had never known why and when his mother died; nor had he any memory of the funeral. Though he could (and even this is conjecture, for who can separate memory and fantasy) picture various very early scenes, the actual death was entirely blank. He first slept with Marie in March, a year and a month before her marriage. The August following their consummation he did, indeed, interrogate Mikhail on matters pertaining to Anna's death. But even this conversation, intense though it was, failed to set off the desired memories. A further confession then (although I hardly intend this journal as a complete memoirs, a few confessions are never out of order): one of the purposes of the occasional lapses into Korsoniloff's earlier life has been to catalyse the memory of that day and answer the crucial question.

I say has been. But no, I am not indulging in a concealed introduction (though doubtless I will when the time comes) for although fragments have returned the whole still escapes me. An impossible project? Not at all, for Mikhail informed me, in the above-mentioned conversation, that I had been three years old and evinced some surprise at my failure to remember.

However, he himself was unable to jog my memory with many details as he, of course, had not been witness to the fatal event; he had been up at the house. The next day, for sundry reasons but mostly for my own protection, he had left me in the care of a baby-sitter for the funeral.

Were I to attempt to locate a point in time, a focal juncture, at which Korsoniloff's actions began to bring about his own downfall, I would have to pick that evening spent with Mikhail and Bess—whom, incidentally, I have not seen since. There was, of course, no formal break, but the nature of the meeting was such that it has seemed wiser not to risk re-opening certain wounds until it is certain that they have been healed. Why then, do I pursue this memory, when the consequences have thus far proved disastrous? First, because I am curious and second because it has been so disastrous. Besides one must inevitably, appropriate and console oneself with one's own history.

'One'. The word is so impersonal and the formulations so abstract. But do people not often become abstract to generalise from their most personal experience? But the question need not be rhetorical. For I am not being abstract for aesthetic reasons, but in order to conceal. Not out of shame or guilt (for how can one be responsible for the actions of one's three year old self?) but out of incompleteness. For I must know all the details, for reasons which must be self-evident, before I can present, or even face myself, what is already known. Enough, for while it may seem I am tantalising you I am tantalising myself more. Nothing could be clearer than that.

Before that visit home in August, Marie and I continued the tranquil period which preceded my discovery about Korsoniloff's drive for self-knowledge. It even began to affect my sleeping schedule. My usual habit, and one which I always returned to, was to stay up late and get up late.

I think I would be an insomniac if I tried to get to sleep at the same time every night and I've seldom felt any great desire to sleep a lot. But for a couple of weeks that August I got into the habit of going to sleep early then waking up early in the morning. After the first day or two it got so I wanted to be awake as soon as it was light out. It was, and for no apparent reason, an optimistic change. I would get up and get dressed and then go to the kitchen for a cup of coffee and a cigarette. Then I would go out for a walk, get my morning paper, and read it. But after a few days I quit reading the paper and went for longer walks instead. I found it was impossible for me to worry about anything, or even think about anything, just watching everything happen. What is commonplace to those who rise at seven every morning is phenomenal to late risers.

Whatever it is that happens early in the morning has never seemed to have much connection with me. Naturally I'm glad someone's out depositing my morning paper in its box, opening banks and toting up my account card, doing my laundry. But still, despite my theoretical knowledge that it affects my life, I find walking around in the morning like looking into a goldfish bowl.

I am insatiably curious about other people's lives. If I were a woman I would be a terrible gossip. And at this period all those people, getting onto buses, walking purposefully on their way to somewhere, fascinated me. I found I divided people into three classes. There were those who were obviously on their way to work or an appointment. They were all respectably dressed, neat and freshly washed. You know by the look on someone's face that they've just gotten up, washed, and eaten breakfast. Their mouth looks as if they're trying

to decide whether the milk in their cereal really was a bit off
or if it just tastes funny mixed with toothpaste. Then there
are the people left over from the night before. They all look
steamrollered. I don't know why staying up a few extra
hours should have such a negative effect on the human coun-
tenance but it does. At five or six in the morning they're con-
tent to go around looking like they're feeling: absolutely
exhausted. But by seven or eight, unhappily surrounded by the
multitudes going to work, their faces take on a guiltier cast.
They try to look, never convincingly, as if they too are on
their way somewhere, doing the socially constructive thing
and taking their place in the business of the world. They forget that they are unshaven and that their clothes are rumpled
and they sit on the buses reading the morning paper and
pretending to look brightly out the window.

And then the third category. They aren't going to work;
you can tell by the way they're dressed. But they aren't left
over from the night before either. Anyone who had retired
from the military or has gotten a disability pension or has a
small inheritance could fall into this category. Or maybe some
who have just read Norman Vincent Peale. If you want to
find these people look in a hardware store between 9 and 10.

And myself? I don't know. Getting up early is an op-
timistic thing to do but I wasn't really feeling that way.
Maybe I just wanted a change. Or to see the limits of where
I live.

Our relationship, though it lost some of the heaviness
which had characterised it, took on no new dynamic. We
slipped into a peaceful, almost vacuous, limbo. Walking through
the streets on hot nights, lying naked on a sheet feeling the
air move around us, meeting occasionally in the afternoon
and lying in the sun, we had nothing to say to each other
and didn't feel the lack. Our intimacy was assumed, based

on silent understandings and mutual innuendoes of contentment. Does it seem I was at peace? I must have been. But if I was, I wasn't ready for it. Korsoniloff, satisfied, was restless. I could yield to Korsoniloff but he couldn't seem to give in to himself.

Marie, true to her submissive nature, was never demanding. It was only after months of our affair that I saw this and realised how pliable she was. Even her sensuality represented a surrender to my wishes. The thought irritated me; I imagined grabbing her shoulders and shaking her till the expression on her face went out of control. But how could I? It would have been too out of character. Even Korsoniloff could not do such a thing. Though in fact he did come close on several occasions. One night, drifting in the peacefulness that was imperceptibly moving towards emptiness, choking suddenly, he turned to Marie and made love to her violently testing his hands against the softness of her flesh. At first she was still, then something deep in her responded and we finally established contact, convinced and drawn in by our own fury. Afterwards I lay still on top of her, panting, confused and guilty. Not so much at my own behaviour as the response it brought out in her. Nothing was said; what had happened so contradicted our unspoken myths that it couldn't be recognised.

In that something snapped for me. Illusion to reality? Hardly. But I ceased to want her as a part of me. We had been differentiated. But I had no desire to stop seeing her; I had only been made aware that the limbo we were in could not extend without limit.

XI

Although I spend a lot of time thinking I don't regard myself, even Korsoniloff aside, as an intellectual. At one time, more than ten years ago, I wanted to become a philosopher. I can remember sitting at my desk reading texts and endless commentaries. Orderly preparation for an orderly future. But then something snapped. It was in graduate school; I was studying for my comprehensive examinations. In front of me were folders full of notes and summaries made over the preceding few years. I realised that while I had thought I was studying philosophy, in reality I had become a clerk. The student in me resisted. After all, had I not spent years studying the history of philosophical thought? Had I not been exposed to some of the greatest minds in history? Surely something must have rubbed off. Some desire for truth or at least rigour. At least some modes of reasoning must have become open to me. But the clichés seemed flimsy. What did I know? I knew who said what when and what someone else said to refute it. My task had been to memorise the minutes of philosophical thought and learn how to give a credible imitation. How had it affected my experience except to remove me from it?

Once disengaged from the illusion that I had been nur-

turing my mind towards profundity I asked myself if I wanted
to be profound. I couldn't answer that question for I had
neither any idea of what profound meant nor any desire to
find out.

Theories of existence were of no use to me. I couldn't
even experience my own life. I took a cardboard carton from
my shelf and started clearing my desk into it. Not only had I
learned nothing from philosophy—I was also learning nothing
by rejecting it.

I wondered what to do. I didn't want to become a bus
conductor or a prospector. I still, for the sake of the fringe
benefits, wanted to teach university. If I couldn't promise any
truth beyond banality at least I wouldn't pretend to have a
secret key to esoterica. Fuck it. I would be what I was. A
competent second-rate historian.

Although I've suffered brief relapses I doubt that I've
read more than ten books in my field in the last six years. I
read the journals that come into my office—including the book
reviews—and consult my notes. To some it might seem strange
that a professional teacher of philosophy could regard his job
in such a light. Actually I think it must be quite common.

I've often thought about that night. I try to remember
what it was that held me to philosophy before it. And how
something that had motivated me so strongly could have dissolved so easily. Sometimes I've tried to get inside the minds
of some of my more inspired students, to re-experience through
them whatever it was I must have felt. But it's impossible. I
can no longer imagine what it would be like to desire knowledge,
or to think that it holds something of value. To be sure I
still think and analyse, introspect and tear to pieces. But that,
it seems, is more from habit than conviction. A grid to filter
and distance reality.

When I finished putting my books away I was still disappointed. If I was doomed to precocious senility as an intellectual then I wanted compensation. Boredom would be even worse than ignorance. If one was going to live—live fully, I had always thought. Now that was meaningless verbiage. If I had to live through my alienated self I was in no position to strike a superior bargain. It was Korsoniloff or nothing. I took Korsoniloff. Or tried to.

When I got back to Toronto after seeing Mikhail and Bess last August my restlessness got much more acute. At first I thought it was my usual hesitations about another year of teaching, then it melted in with the increasing tensions with Marie. But instead of being thoroughly in the midst of it I felt like the container of an unknown process. My habit of early rising broke down immediately when I couldn't sleep at night; I would sit in a chair by Marie's window staring out or watching her sleep. It's a funny thing about those hours; alone and not even knowing what kept me awake, I had a strange fraternal feeling. In the night, by an open window, you hear a lot of sounds. People on the street, laughter, crying, cats, cars. Listening there, perhaps because I was so disconnected from myself, I would imagine what it would be like to be in the position of those making the sounds. The occasional weeping from the house next door brought me near to understanding why a woman cries. No, not understanding; feeling what she feels.

There is, late at night in that empathetic solitude, a murderous blankness. With the feelings so tightly sealed one can do anything; really, I've never quite trusted overly composed people. In any case there is no need to describe these moments, for aside from hunger and desire the experience must be one of the most commonly known.

I would remain there, by the window, one part of me

containing Korsoniloff's stewing, until dawn. Then having, for lack of a better resolution, waited it out, I would go to sleep. When I woke Marie would have left. Still withdrawn in a residual way—slowed down by it to a pseudo-calm—I would go back to my place and set about doing whatever I had to do that day. Some days, it was September, there would be meetings. Occasionally I would look over notes and think about the year's lectures. But most afternoons I just walked about, enjoying the last bit of summer.

After a while I developed a ritual. I would wake up about eleven. Then I would pick up a morning paper and a cinnamon bun at a bakery on Harbord Street. At home I would read the paper and have the bun with coffee. It had been a while since I had read the paper regularly; at first I just looked at the sports and the comics but soon I was reading it from cover to cover. It generated, I don't mean this cynically, a sense of utter powerlessness. Out there (wherever there is) were occurring all sorts of complex events—generally bringing misery to the people involved. At the same time that I observed the world through the newspaper it occurred to me that everywhere, in thousands and millions and hundreds of millions of chairs, were sitting people reading their newspapers and digesting earthquakes, wars and propaganda along with their buns.

All this began to affect Marie. She became, despite our occasional outbursts of violence, intuitively resigned. I spied on her impending inner collapse not knowing if I dreaded it or wanted it. When she finally reacted I was unprepared. I had come over one night half-wanting to see her and half-wishing that I had something else to do, that being with Marie hadn't obliterated the other things, so that when she came to the door looking like she'd been crying I assumed it was something else and asked what was the matter. She didn't reply of course but suggested going for a walk. It was early fall and

61

still warm in the evenings so we began walking, my attention given over to the air and thoughts about the impending winter. We ended up in a park, sitting on the grass. She looked at me and told me that before she had met me she had known no one deeply and had felt alone within herself but that now she felt not only alone but isolated and that she wasn't sure but that she preferred the first. When she said that I felt, although guilty, relieved. I suppose it was my ambivalence that was keeping us out of contact, or so I thought, and I began to try to reassure her without being overly dishonest.

It was, then, just as well that she cut me off by saying she wouldn't believe anything I said and didn't want to see me any more. At first it seemed an attractive idea. After all, what did I do but sit up nights listening to the darkness. For a few seconds I pictured myself doing the same things without her. Perhaps what she suggested would be for the best. Korsoniloff's ardour was becoming exhausted and I had nothing to replace it with. I felt myself shaping a few well-rounded sentences in my mind to expedite matters.

Look at me, she said. Look at me when you talk. I looked at her without saying anything. I looked at her more closely. They say that when you look into a person's eyes you can gain great insights. I looked into her eyes. They were brown with black flecks. The flecks were almost impossible to see and if I hadn't first noticed them when we were making love I wouldn't have seen them again. I kissed her. Not here she said. It was dark. It was a big park. I kissed her again. Finally we went back to her place and though we both worried about it the walk didn't kill it.

Korsoniloff began to have a strong need to preserve his equilibrium against Marie. It's strange how we were dominated by the tacit myths of our relationship. We had played our roles in coming together so tightly that our knowledge of each other was assumed. With Gail, on the contrary, I'd make no such assumption. This must be a common experience but it's not to me; a relationship which exists behind personalities. Really, that's how Gail knows me; she knows how to neutralise my various quirks. If Marie aroused me by wanting to be fulfilled, Gail makes it possible, at least for brief periods, to be aside from all that. Whatever it is I do for her I have no idea. I gather that she has no desire to be known—at least by me.

XII

Gail.

I was blank, empty, nothing. I had nothing to say and wanted to say it at great length. I asked her for a pen and paper and started writing nothing over and over again. First very neatly, three lines of nothing. Then in bigger writing, two lines high, ten lines of nothing. Then a big Nothing right to the bottom of the page. Finally, over the other side of the page a big N covering the whole page and on top of it an O and on top of it a T and on top of it a

Tell me a story.

I don't know any stories.

Tell me a story.

Samuel Spoltroon, resident of 114th street, living in a purple-doored house with a swimming-pool-blue persian carpet at the front entrance put, one day, seven green threads in the right breast pocket of his black and grey double-breasted made-over suit and set out down the street in search of a candle. After a brief walk he came to a great brass archway with ornate inlaid figures of serpents, angels and other occult designs which he stared at for a long time trying to figure out whether they were hand carved or merely stamped on before asking the resident Troll, a dark figure with a cloudy beard, what he had to do to get through the archway. Why do you want to pass through here said the Troll sucking ominously on his snakeskin pipe.

Samuel answered that he was looking for a candle.

Very well said the Troll, then in order to pass through these gates on your highly symbolic search you must be carrying a flame.

But, Samuel protested, I don't have a flame; that is why I am looking for a candle. But the Troll could not be dissuaded. After all, he told Samuel, everyone knows that there is no way of going on a symbolic mission without carrying a flame.

So Samuel, properly chastened, decided that he would return home to get a flame and re-commence his search hoping to have better luck. He thought that maybe he would bring his brand new shiny silver propane pipe lighter with an adjustable flame and an eleven speed gearbox. But when he turned around to start back down the street he found that it wasn't there; instead he was on a path which ran beside a clear stream. Suspecting foul play Samuel took out of the breast pocket of his made-over double-breasted suit a green thread and hung it over a branch in a shrub so that he could find his way back. Then after washing his hands in the clear stream, it seemed to be the thing to do, he set out down the path hoping for the best.

Walking down the path beside the clear stream Samuel felt an inexplicable sense of well-being which he attributed to the mission he had undertaken. Taking out his purple silk handkerchief he blew his nose and shook his head around vigorously. Then, refreshed, he bent down and tightened the buckles of his black boots by one notch each. He wiped the

65

shoes with the clean side of his handkerchief and threw it away. Despite his difficulties Samuel Spoltroon was still an expansive man. As he walked along, enjoying the fine weather, Samuel noticed that the path was getting thinner and thinner and that the undergrowth was getting thicker and thicker. Just as he began to think that he had gotten lost in the forest, though to tell the truth he had suspected that something like this might happen, he came to a clearing. At one edge of the clearing, guarding the bridge that ran over the stream which had, behind the bush that made it invisible, become a torrent, was a small old man with long white hair though the crown of his head was bald. He sat, cross-legged, Samuel identified it as a half-lotus, not quite lost in contemplation for he was watching Samuel's approach.

Good morning Samuel, the old man said, what brings you here?

Good morning father, Samuel replied, listening to himself. I seem to be on a mission to find a candle. Could I cross the bridge and continue my search?

Well, said the old man, you can cross the bridge if you can answer one question.

Shoot father.

Here it is. Tell me your name that I do not know.

Crazylegs, shouted Samuel, taking a run at the old man and hurdling over him onto the bridge landed in stride and was well into his fourth step when a wind swept him over the bridge and he found himself falling towards the river. Well, thought Samuel, I can't be blamed for trying. Having already revealed his latent athletic skills he had no hesitation in starting to swim shortly after he splashed into the water. He soon became accustomed to its temperature, which he didn't find as cold as he had feared, and began looking about for a place to go ashore. The growth about the banks of the river

was so thick that for a moment he despaired of finding a
clear place to crawl ashore but then, in a sudden interplay of
shadows, he spotted a lip of rock and earth that seemed to
be just what he was looking for. He swam up to it and pulled
himself onto the ledge. Extracting a collapsible hanger from
his right front coat pocket he hung up his made-over double-
breasted suit on it and placed that on a near-by tree branch.
Then he took off his terylene shirt and brass buckle shoes and
clad only in his jockey undershorts and elastihose sat down to
regain his wind. Of the bridge, he must have been swept
around a bend, he could see nothing, so feeling very tired and
not knowing what else to do he lay down and fell immediately
into a deep sleep.

When he awoke it was night-time. For the first time, for
Samuel Spoltroon didn't scare easily, he knew he was frightened.
He reached up for his shirt but couldn't find it. Nor his shoes
nor his suit. It was too dark. He had heard of people looking
at the stars to estimate the time. He looked up at the sky; it
was brilliant—he had never seen the stars so clearly before. But
there was no hint of the time. There seemed, at least for a
moment, to be a shimmering of light on one horizon, he hoped
desperately but without conviction that it might be the start
of the dawn, but after staring at it for a while he began to
wonder if it was really there anyway. Well, he thought, nothing can happen to me and in a few hours it will be light. Then
I can swim up the river and climb the bank and apologise to
the old man and maybe he'll tell me how to get home. So,
satisfied that his plan would see him through successfully, he
decided that the sensible thing to do was to go back to sleep
until dawn, especially as being awake was kind of spooky.
But when he lay down again he couldn't sleep. He couldn't
even stay lying down. The rock was bumpy and uncomfortable.
Behind the rock were some big shrubs. Perhaps there would be

67

a clear space of earth behind them. But instead of finding a place to sleep he discovered something else. The shrubs were just a kind of camouflage to the entrance to a cave. Hm, Samuel said, this is certainly a coincidence. Maybe he would be able to sleep in the cave. He crawled through the shrubs into the cave. It was warmer but not too damp. He thought it must be pretty small; it looked as if the back was only a few feet off. But wary of snakes and whatever else it is that bothers people about caves Samuel decided to leave exploration until daylight and get some sleep.

He was too nervous to lie down. He slumped with his back against one wall and didn't expect to sleep; nonetheless he lost consciousness almost as quickly as he had that afternoon. He began to dream weird noises and rustlings, then, in the dream, it was silent. Then there was a set of footfalls. A lantern-carrying man in a grey cloak was standing above him looking at him. Then the man sat down, apparently to wait. Samuel, watching himself dream, kept feeling that he ought to wake up. But though he tried to rouse himself he could not. After all, even if awake, how could he defend himself? It was all too much and he stayed asleep. When he awoke he looked around. The man in the cloak was standing on the rock looking at the water. Samuel got up and stretched. He went out to find his clothes. They were gone. Excuse me, he said, but you haven't seen my clothes have you? The man turned towards Samuel. The hood to his cloak was contrived so that his face always remained half-shadowed.

No, said the man, I didn't. But there was a strong wind last night; perhaps they were carried away. Samuel didn't say anything. When he had fallen asleep the night had been clear and still. He looked about where the clothes had been. He found his pants and shirt hooked to adjoining shrubs. There was no sign of anything else. It did look as if they might have been blown away by a wind.

The man drew a greasy paper bag from his cloak and took out some bread. Here, he said to Samuel, take this.

Raisin Bread! he exclaimed, eating the whole slice in a tremendous gulp. Without explaining the man led Samuel back into the cave and relit his lantern. In the light Samuel could see that it extended indefinitely. He took a couple of steps but then stopped. Having no shoes was going to be a problem. As if this had been anticipated—by this time Samuel was so suspicious he didn't even bother thinking about it—the man drew out a pair of hush-puppy all-weather moccasins and handed them to him. They fitted. Well, said Samuel, recapturing his usual good humour. If the cap fits wear it ha ha ha.

The man said nothing and commenced to lead him into the cave. After about half an hour's walking through the increasingly twisting passageways the man put his hand on Samuel's shoulder indicating that he should stop. Then he began walking about, lighting, from his own, lanterns which were placed at intervals about what was taking shape as a definite room-like area. As the last lanterns were lit Samuel noticed a definite increase in the warmth of the reflected colour; a golden throne was revealed. On one side was the Troll, idly swinging a brass watch-fob. On the other was the old man. His long hair was held up and being plaited by the beautiful woman who sat upon the throne. She sat there, beautiful and abundant, smiling forgivingly at Samuel.

XIII

Well, she said, in an indescribable voice.

Yes, said Samuel.

Can I be of service to you?

Samuel, knowing that the moment was upon him, looked around the room. He didn't seem to be able to concentrate on her question. He seemed, without doubt, to be the most nervous person in the room. He felt nervous.

Are you nervous?, she asked.

It was too much to reply. I don't know, he said. No one else said anything at all though he was sure that they all knew that he was the most nervous person in the room. He thought he'd better say something. It's a nice cave you have here. You'd never know it from the outside.

Still no one said anything. Samuel was beginning to feel conspicuous. He realised that he was soon going to have to go to the bathroom. He was sure they hadn't passed one on the way. Had he known what was going to happen he would have stopped to pee before the man had lit the lanterns. Of course he could always pee in his pants, no one would notice, it was too dark. Still, no one else seemed to need to pee.

Go ahead, she said, I would if I were you.

Her saying that made him twitch uncontrollably. By the time he had stopped twitching he realised he had wet himself. There was no doubt about it; he was the most nervous person in the room.

I'm not sure I should be here said Samuel. He was still standing up. His legs felt tired and his left leg felt clammy. Everyone else seemed to be sitting down. Even the cloaked man had found some kind of stool.

I seem to be nervous, Samuel said.

Yes.

Maybe I'd feel better if I could sit down. He looked around. There didn't seem to be anything to sit on.

Why don't you sit on my lap?

No, Samuel shouted. No thanks. He sat down on the floor. It wasn't so bad after all. Actually he sat a couple of paces away from where he had been standing, just for safety's sake. They were all sitting now. They weren't a bad group, the four of them. He still felt a bit out of place but figured that would pass when his leg dried. He looked around some more. He wished he could remember a good joke or something to put everyone at their ease. Somewhere at the back of his mind something was nagging at him. Oh yes, her question.

Actually, Samuel said, I'm looking for something.

Yes, the woman said plentifully.

I think I'm looking for a candle.

I could give you one, if that's what you want.

Samuel began to feel nervous again. No one else did. He wished he had thought to ask the cloaked man for one. He seemed to have everything else. He had the feeling that if he just got a candle and left he would be missing out on something. Besides, he wasn't really sure how to get home. On the other hand he didn't know what else to ask for. Perhaps something to eat but that didn't seem appropriate. He looked at the woman longingly. He thought there was something apocryphal about her. He wondered what apocryphal meant. He asked her. What does apocryphal mean? The little old man pulled a dictionary from under the throne. He wondered what else they kept there.

Apocryphal, he read, of doubtful authenticity.

Perhaps, Samuel said slowly, I think there's something apocryphal about this situation. The woman smiled. The Troll twirled. The old man moved his head with the plaiting motions of the woman. The man with the lantern sat and did nothing at all.

On the other hand, he allowed, perhaps it is my presence here that is apocryphal. Nothing happened.

Or, he posited, perhaps it is our relation that is apocryphal. There was a hiss and a puff of mauve smoke. Samuel found himself sitting on the steps of his house on 114th street. In his hand was a black candle. It was burning.

Well? said Gail.

The moral of the story is: look before you leap.

No, not that.

What?

She put her hand on my leg. It felt funny; we started to laugh.

Let's look at the clocks, I said. We went into the room and looked at them. I kept looking around the room trying to find one to focus on. But I didn't seem to be able to concentrate. My leg still felt funny. I decided I wanted to take a bath. I started running the water and looking around the bathroom. I decided to trim my beard first. I started to grow it the day I turned 21. Every now and then I trim it, sometimes a slightly different shape for variety. I was feeling somewhat pointy so I decided to trim it to a point. I snipped enough hair off till the chin looked like a goatee. In the living-room Gail was lying on the couch suggestively leafing through a book of Botticelli prints. How do you like it? I asked.

It looks terrible.

I went back to the bathroom. It was true; I looked terrible. I snipped and trimmed until patches of skin showed at the cheeks. Then I took her razor and shaved the sides of my face. The skin was tender and more pale than the rest of my face. I washed my face several times and went back into the living-room. How does this look, I asked.

It looks great.

I went back to the bathroom. It was true; I looked great. I got into the bath and sank completely underwater except for my nose and my knees. My face didn't feel even. I got out and looked into the mirror. Then I shaved off the rest of my beard and got into the bath.

I felt numb. Walled in. I wanted to relax but I was too numb to be able to. I sat and thought about the different things I could do. I didn't really want to make love. Or eat. Or read. I didn't even seem to want to be in the bath but there was no reason to move. I decided to try to go to sleep. I couldn't sleep; the water was too cold. I ran some more hot water and tried again. It still didn't feel right. I didn't even have enough energy to be restless. I got up and looked in the mirror again. I hadn't really seen what I was doing before. My face looked weird. There were red blotches everywhere and little patches where the beard hairs still showed. My face seemed tiny compared to my hair. One sideburn was longer than the other. I trimmed the long one so that they were both halfway down my ears. I wondered if I would be sorry tomorrow when I shaved. I went into the living-room dripping.

73

Gail stared at me and I felt naked. I went and lay down in the bedroom. Finally Gail came in and started rubbing my back: I still felt numb but began to think I could sleep.

Gail seemed so calm rubbing my back, lying beside me. I began to be aware of how naked I was. I wasn't wearing anything at all. I sat up, drawing the sheet up to my navel. Gail lay there looking calm. Had the urge to shut the light and make love. Almost as if I wanted to hide inside her. I put the soles of my feet against each other. Started hearing popping sounds. As if little bubbles in my head were popping. Energy seemed to be passing through the air, through my head, and through the other side. I wanted to lose myself in its flow but couldn't. Gail was lying on her stomach, her face in the pillow. She might have been asleep. I decided to cross my legs and meditate on my navel. I thought about my navel. The skin there began to feel tender; I thought if I touched it, it would hurt. Gail turned over so I knew she was awake. I asked her to touch me there. She did; I knew she was going to and saw her stretching her hand towards me but when she touched me I still jumped.

I got up and put on my pants and walked into the living-room. Who was I being, André or Korsoniloff? Of course, in a sense, intellectually, I realise that I am neither and both. But what is that kind of intellectual cognisance? A concession to someone else's reality. A deduction of what must be the case. Since I am I and am all that I am I must be all my forms. Very neat. But I didn't feel it. As Korsoniloff satisfied there was never this sense of restlessness. And I wouldn't otherwise have any interest in this situation. I felt trapped in thought patterns that I'd made too complicated to unravel. Very well; I wouldn't attempt to. I made some coffee and flipped through a couple of art books. They bored me and I put them away. I read the help-wanted section of the newspaper. You could make a lot of money as a computer programmer.

I remembered having shaved my beard and went in and looked in the mirror again. The skin on my cheeks seemed to have been spared the last decade. I should have grown a beard under my eyes. The skin around your eyes tells you the effect of what you have seen. They looked stony cold. I smiled and they were anomalous. I looked at myself looking at myself. In my eyes I could see a reflection of my face. I wished I could see more clearly so that I could follow the image through every reflection.

I walked back into the bedroom and looked at Gail. She was lying in bed pretending to sleep. I didn't have any idea of what was going on in her head. I never did. She seemed absolutely self-contained and without need. It was as if I paid her for whatever she did for me and she had her real life elsewhere. She never seemed bothered if she couldn't see me but she was always glad when I was free. If I phoned her she was almost always available. If I didn't want to see her for a few days she didn't mind and didn't ask questions. If I was passive she would be active. If I was active she would respond to whatever I did. She was the perfect closed system.

I looked at her body on the bed. It had no faults. Her flesh is firm without being lumpy. She is graceful but not conspicuous. She lifted her head and looked me 20-20 straight in the eye hiding nothing, revealing less. She asked me if I wanted to come to bed. I don't feel like it, I said.

She asked me if I wanted something to eat. I said I didn't. Okay, she said, smiling perfectly and closing her eyes. I sat down beside her and looked under her eyes. There was 1 lower eyelid for each one.

XIV

I have started hearing voices. The controls must be getting confused. It's somehow satisfying to have something definite like that happen. It began a couple of weeks ago. I was walking home from Gail's looking at apartment buildings sticking up into the sky. The total potential energy available for jumping seemed very dangerous. An uneasy thought.

Then there was a faint sound—my name—I turned and looked, sure someone was calling. But I couldn't see anyone. I walked back a few steps, listening, and then gave up. All that day I was preoccupied with the sound and listened to the radio news that night. Then, as I was drifting asleep, it happened again. This time it could be heard more distinctly—the clear, high-pitched voice of a woman. Was she calling for help? It seemed so but there was something else in it—perhaps a note of revenge, which warned me.

Now sometimes there are shouts and confused mumblings. But I can never make out the words; if I try to concentrate on them they fade away.

Clarence came down to return some books he had borrowed. He said he had seen me coming and going in Gail's car and wondered if she was my girl friend. I didn't say anything; I was hoping he would leave so I could get some sleep but he ignored the hint and sat down to talk. Patsy had gotten to him with a joke about his studies and he had been brooding about it ever since. Not that he was the type to worry; in fact he said he never did. But maybe there was something to what she said. He wasn't sure he wanted to be an accountant and work in an office all the time. He didn't like being looked down upon, and maybe respectability was the main factor after all.

I had no idea how to respond. I wondered what Gail would do if she were here. I wondered what I would do. Actually I regretted my own respectability.

If that's what you want maybe it doesn't matter why you're doing it.

Clarence waited for me to continue. I felt inane.

On the other hand maybe that's what's most important after all.

I was saved by a knock on the door and Patsy's entrance. I invited her in and poured everyone a drink. Patsy and Clarence had obviously had quite an argument. They directed their comments about the weather towards me while I was left to feel out some sort of solution. I didn't know what to do. I said so. We all chuckled briefly and then fell into total silence. It occurred to me that they weren't looking for advice but just wanted someplace handy to go and have a drink. And I had a whole bottlefull.

After a couple more drinks I began to feel woozy and lay down. By this time Patsy and Clarence were talking to each other; I didn't notice them leave.

When I looked at myself in the mirror this morning I knew I needed to buy a razor and some razor blades. I used to have a rusty razor but I'd thrown it out a long time ago. When I got back I shaved and looked so smooth and gaunt

I wondered where I came from.

Maybe the voices really were the start of something. Or were they? I expect disaster but maybe I can't reach ground zero. Maybe everything just comes back together in some unexpected way.

I got caught once smoking a cigar in the basement of the school. They used to make us do the turkey dance. Maybe because it sounded too funny to complain about. You get lifted just off the ground, gripped around the upper arm, and moved very rapidly back and forth feet trotting trying to keep up   touch the ground to relieve the pressure. For a few hours afterwards, if it was the right arm, it was very hard to throw a ball. Or to write but that was never considered sufficient excuse.

It seems funny to be wanting to collapse so badly. To have everything reduced to its simplest state.

I'm tired of responsible reality. Of the endless perambulations and qualifications that shrink every action to a size convenient for handling and rationalisation. What I want is

Were they or weren't they? The external events don't bother me too much. It's the endless stream of trivial questions. Do this, do that. Have you examined every aspect of everything or is it still moving?

Poor baby.

And the gut is where it's all taken in. From the first day you're born—you know children aren't trained by memory work—the process begins. The gut is jammed into patterns. Stamped and moulded. Dumping grounds for obscene ideologies are cleared. Passageways are twisted and contorted so that the slightest deviation will produce terror and pain and thus normalisation. Controls.

I never should have gotten involved with Marie. She was

too healthy, too strong for me to handle. By the time we were finished I was so twisted up in myself I couldn't see anything straight. Only my own weakness was left, and a
(Why does it have to happen to me?)
Poor baby.
Maybe I'm afraid to be really insane. Horror story flipout. I'd like a nice quiet middle-class insanity. A tacit agreement not to be taken seriously in return for being allowed to ignore conventional reality. A nice secure volitional catatonia. Everything is completely arbitrary so will is the only real element.

XV

The strain continued to bother Marie. She would get depressed suddenly, without apparent reason. At first I thought it was a reaction to my ambivalence. I became guilty, solicitous. But the more I reached out to her the more she withdrew. It made me very uncomfortable. Every tremor in her disposition was magnified ten times in my own. If she got a slight headache I would have migraine. If she complained of nausea I would end up retching. Within a couple of weeks my pseudo-freedom from her evaporated completely. The more I tried to help the worse things got.

I berated myself to her, apologising a thousand times for the slightest disturbance. My regret was sincere though I wasn't sure whether it was my fault. But what I lacked in humility Marie made up. It was true, all true; she agreed with everything and added a few innovations of her own. I was too harsh, cruel, callous, cold, uncaring, demanding. Our attention shifted from her depressions to my inadequacy. She took upon herself, generously, the burden of raising me from my sub-human level of existence.

We began what she called my 'self-improvement' campaign. Every time I said or did something that was potentially injurious to her she would point it out and I would try to figure out how I could have done such a thing. Since I was generally unable to understand even the erroneous nature of what I had done Marie would have to help me. She did. She was unremittingly helpful. No one could have been more patient. A devotee of psychology, she analysed the roots, developments and manifestations of my hostility towards women, especially her. As she herself once explained, why should I have to go through life handicapped with unnecessary blocks? Why indeed? In the face of her analyses I felt my emotional development must have stopped at about age three. It was too much for me to handle. After two weeks of the campaign I cracked.

I told her I couldn't take it. Not at all. Every true Christian must bear his burden and I was willing to shoulder mine. She explained that I was showing resistance, which was a good sign. My hostility towards the program was just a defence mechanism and I should confront it directly. I said that I wanted to but I couldn't. I don't remember the details of the rest of the discussion, but at the end it was agreed that the campaign was over or at least indefinitely suspended.

When she announced for the second time that she thought we ought to stop seeing each other I tried to change her mind. Not because the time we spent together was so good— in fact it was not. But because I wanted to resolve whatever it was in me that was contributing to the general mess. I was hooked on the idea of my own psychological progress. Marie sensed it but was adamant. There was a point in the conversation when I felt absolutely poised on the precipice. If I once more insisted that we keep seeing each other, she would agree on the condition that we resume the campaign. But if I could get her to say 'I'm sorry but my mind is made up' once more I would be free of the whole thing and could.

walk out with a suitably injured look on my face. The moment, sliced out of time, pulled Korsoniloff away from its context. Just as he was about to pull himself back to the business of making a decision Marie appeared with his coat.

It seemed so appropriate there was nothing else to do. Put on the coat, smile benignly, and start to the door. At the head of the stairs I hesitated. Perhaps it was all a bluff. Perhaps we were carrying through our motions by rote, not really thinking about what we were doing but just impelled by the momentum of what had already happened. It was an unfortunate thought. It imparted a whole sense of arbitrariness to what was happening. Events, especially decisive ones, should never appear arbitrary. They should be absolutely certain and unavoidable. One cannot regret what had to be.

I wanted to say to her 'Marie this is silly, we don't have to play this game.' I turned to face her but she was no longer there.

I snuck downstairs feeling dissatisfied. Had I just walked straight out to begin with, played my assigned part in the drama with dignity and stoic calm, I could have left with a sense of self-righteous satisfaction. As it was I was left strung out and hanging.

I knew it was ridiculous. Couldn't I just pretend that Korsoniloff had, indeed, performed as expected? Who was to know? Even Marie had probably not seen the hesitation; she had certainly not seen me turn right around. But what if she had merely seen me hesitate, and then slipped out of sight so I couldn't face her? She had really done it to me. Taken no chances and lost nothing.

I played it over and over in my mind for days. But no matter how I looked at it, it seemed the same. I tried to persuade myself that it was impossible that Marie would run around telling people that Korsoniloff had lost his nerve and hesitated. And even if she did, what did it matter? I realised how deeply Korsoniloff had been sucked into the whole thing. And why not? For was Korsoniloff not the opposite of detachment? There was no doubt. Marie had played him perfectly.

The more I thought about it the more I wanted to some-how reverse the situation. I fantasised meeting her and being so aloof that she would have to try to break down the barriers. At which point Korsoniloff, with a shrug of the shoulders and a look of unconcealed embarrassment, would leave. Why was revenge necessary? The end result would be the same. But she had tricked Korsoniloff by first torturing him and then making impossible any attempts at reprisal. Once, my voice disguised, I did attempt to telephone her. But she wasn't home and I didn't leave a message.

Involved in my distorted griefs I became more and more obnoxious at the university. Once Korsoniloff took over com-pletely and vented his feelings by calling a student stupid. There was a shocked silence in the class which was only broken when, in the coldest possible voice, I commenced reading from my notes in a monotone and continued until the end of the hour.

When I look back to that period now it is almost with affection. I feel sorry for Korsoniloff duped, despite his feelings of sophistication, by his own unbearable innocence. For weeks he was totally stranded in defeat. Every day he expected a letter from Marie. Every time he went to pick up his mail from the departmental office or his home his heart would accelerate in anticipation of her presence. When his phone rang he would fumble it off the hook, sure that it must be Marie.

By the time she finally did phone he had convinced him-self that she wouldn't and was surprised to hear her voice.

Forgetting his planned aloofness he eagerly agreed to a meeting. She took about an hour to get there. He was very nervous and ended up emptying the ash tray twice before she arrived.

She gave him her coat, as if she didn't know where it went, and sat down primly in the armchair. I sat opposite her wondering why she had called—something which hadn't occurred to me while I was waiting for her. Or rather I must have assumed that she wanted to start seeing me again for when she said that she had just come over to talk I felt disappointed. We talked. She talked. She sat there looking very lovely and self-possessed and talked about the various things she was feeling. I soon lost track of what she was saying and watched her mouth moving. I'll never forget it. Her jaw was moving up and down with slow regularity. Her lips expanded and contracted. At intervals she would part them and show her teeth, which are perfectly white and even. Once or twice she laughed, in a mock self-conscious way and I laughed with her. After a while it all stopped happening and she awaited my response.

I can see how you would feel that way, I said understandingly. Her mouth moved briefly in acknowledgement.

As you know I'm not entirely in accord with your point of view. But then, each to his or her own.

She sat there watching me look at her. Actually the more I looked at her the less sure I was that she was entirely self-possessed. In fact she seemed a bit nervous. I thought maybe she wanted to go to bed with me. I wanted to go to bed with her.

Let's go to bed, I said.

You haven't listened to a word I've said, she said redundantly.

But she didn't really care that I hadn't for she came

over, took me by the hand, and led me to the bed. We both wanted to. It was good, not a bittersweet ironic farewell in the least. Afterwards we went out to a restaurant and had spaghetti. We both had good appetites and talked about the different things we were doing. It was only walking her home that I began to wonder what was going to happen. She said goodbye at the door and I didn't have to ask if she wanted to meet with me again. A few days later, unsure again, I telephoned her, and asked if she wanted to meet. She said no, she was busy, and didn't mention anything about another time. This time the sense of loss was diminished. I felt alone but not entirely defeated. The process of numbing seemed to have set in.

The relief, however partial, freed me slightly. I bought a car and spent all my free time out of town. I would drive north in the afternoon and find a place to walk. After an hour or so I would look for a place to sit quietly. By the time the sun set I would be totally chilled and start the drive home; stomach permitting, I would stop at a restaurant along the way. I usually got home by nine. When it finally started to snow seriously I sold the car.

XVI

But she was still inside me, in my gut, fixed between the navel and the diaphragm, a toxic insert forced to the center of my system. I found someone to sleep with but my insides took such a beating that I didn't try it again. Sometimes it was just a dull ache; that was the best because I could just forget it. Other times when it seemed to disappear—to be truly gone—I could laugh flex sleep be myself. But then, suddenly, it would recur. So the times of real freedom became impeded by the fear of their termination. It was omnipresent. I took it for walks, fed it, attempted to exorcise it, changed my mind and tried to assimilate it. Played with it, tortured it, tried to pray to it, ignored it and suffocated in it.

But it was only that spring morning, with the gift of the mandala, that it finally exploded through me, suffused me entirely, ran through my veins and left me.

Wouldn't it be beautiful if once freed it was impossible to be trapped again. The therapeutic apocalypse complete and final for all time in all time.

But the event, even if not final, was gratefully received. And the gratitude remains. Gail called; I told her that for the next few days—until the trial, it has finally come round— I wanted to be alone. As usual she was compliant.

I feel like doing nothing but eating reading and sleeping.

XVII

I woke up this morning to the sound of my name. The voice, a woman's or perhaps an adolescent boy's, clear from all implication called me to nothing but wakefulness. It is, in fact, the penultimate day. The presence in my stomach is still dozing. It is not as bad this time, not as bad at all. At least in a limited sense. For in another sense it is worse. It is a cannibal presence, a narcissus reaper. And the prey? Korsoniloff of course. Korsoniloff being digested by his failures and insufficiencies. Korsoniloff who could not survive the consequences of his own existence.

I once told Gail about Korsoniloff. It was a drowsy morning, we were lying in bed too lazy to get up. I had just woken; she brought me some coffee. I didn't want it—I wasn't sure I wanted to be awake at all. I had been dreaming about two swimmers—one the coach and one the pupil. He was being trained for the Olympics and had succeeded, in the trials, in winning a berth on the team. The coach, however, had a trick up his sleeve. He claimed he was the better swimmer and appealed to me to judge which of them was superior. They decided to race two lengths of the pool. At the beginning it was obvious that the coach had, as he said, superior skill. He was far more powerful and almost machine-like churning through the water. But by the end of the first length

87

the pupil was already ahead and as they swam the second
length he pulled even farther into the lead and finally won
by a good margin. During the race my sympathies, first with
the coach, shifted to the pupil.

I was trying to make sense of the dream and began to
talk about Korsoniloff. Essentially unwhole, without judgement,
he was in the position of having either to serve me or be
destroyed. Even this set of alternatives did not represent a
potential decision—it was just his situation.

Who was the master and who the pupil? I could see it
both ways. For not only did I create Korsoniloff; Korsoniloff's
existence also transformed me. Possibly the relationship
between Korsoniloff and myself was itself susceptible to great
change. With Marie I was, as it were, Korsoniloff. With Gail
there was no such certainty. It's even uncertain that I exist
in any particular way for her. She brings me coffee obediently
but she isn't obeying me, for I never command.

I tell her this and she says nothing. I ask her why she
bothered to bring it to me and she replies that she was having
some herself and it was no trouble. It is impossible to argue, I
am just picking a fight, everything flows through her and she
is untouched.

In retrospect it doesn't matter that I drank the coffee and
quit worrying about the dream. Despite the theoretical vari-
ations Korsoniloff's fate is already decided. Tomorrow, should
he survive, he will be ruled upon. But his sentence is already
being enacted. My stomach feels heavy, a little swollen in fact.
As if I'd eaten several large meals every day for a week. There
are the occasional rumblings of digestion and realignment. If
I sit very still I can feel what seems to be a gnawing. Until I
began to feel it, to sense the swelling and finally to see it, I
presumed my sense of Korsoniloff's demise was as much a
half-reality as his existence. But how can I, a philosopher

sideswiped by the vagueness of philosophy, deny this empirical evidence?

What does it all mean? Nothing I suppose. There is a simultaneous detachment and mourning. Perhaps this is liberation of a low sort. If so the experience resembles purgatory. For days I have sat watch over my stomach. Sometimes I wonder what will happen when the whole process finishes. I don't know. I don't suppose anything much will have changed. Admittedly, when it began, there was considerable fascination about the possibilities of the conclusion. My own mind, not empty in any mystical sense, feels vacant and dulled. Attempting to protect itself from its own intrusions.

And so I stay in here and wait for Tonker to appear. It's only early morning now so there may be several hours to go—if he's going to come today. Why do I wait? Is waiting a better way to pass the time than doing nothing at all? But waiting is itself no thing, a way to remove myself from the present. Alternately the present holds nothing. So waiting is better than a vacuum.

My journal, honest and dishonest, becomes the record of nothing, gives itself the substance necessary to survive, authenticates my life-task of opportunism.

If the day comes up blank I await the night. Hoping dreams will populate and colour themselves and possibly even allow me to remember them. Perhaps I can write them down and pretend there is something to be deciphered.

But Tonker exists in the world. His girths demand attention and recognition. Five times daily he regenerates himself by sustaining his belly. He can sit at a table devouring fried chickens and salads, sour cream and potatoes, bread smeared with peanut butter. Without his belly Tonker would be nothing. With it he confronts the world. In the morning he wakes up and is conscious of hunger. He licks his lips and rubs

89

his hand against his cheeks. Then he eats. When he has eaten, perhaps so successfully that the protuberance is enlarged, he begins to contemplate evacuation. If he does he will feel somehow completed and fulfilled. If he doesn't he can feel the labours and constrictions of his overloaded intestines. Perhaps a momentous fart will escape, alerting all to his predicament and his glory. He decides to wait.

He buttons on his suit, the shirt tucked firmly into the waistband of his trousers, and proceeds to his office on foot. He has a good solid step, the better to feel the definiteness of his weight and to be reminded at each moment of his accomplishment. He works in a tall building; its elevators spare him the embarrassment of his disadvantaged wind. Sometimes he wants to think it is strained with his weight. Otherwise it is smooth and efficient. Its smoothness provides a feeling of complementary power.

When Korsoniloff stands beside Tonker his height becomes puniness. He feels pushed up beyond the natural. Freakily insubstantial.

Tonker pauses upon entering his office. The secretaries—such a man must have several—register the reshaping of the room around his bulk. Satisfied that their vision has been corrected Tonker goes to his inner sanctum, his throne room, his environmentalised chair. He surveys the pile of paperwork on his desk, his externalised monument. He could never sit down in front of one or two onionskin sheets.

As he surveys the shape of his morning a secretary comes in carrying a tray. A glass of orange juice, four sugar-glazed donuts, a pot of coffee, a thick pitcher of cream. Tonker has perhaps once received a silver pitcher as a gift. It is hidden in the bottom drawer of his personal files. He has neither time nor patience for the weakness or delicacy of unformed objects. His hands are big, fat even on the back. Only the length of his fingers prevents them from being impossibly pudgy. Looking at his hands he grasps the food in front of him. The fingers of his left hand implant themselves in the donut. With his right he holds the pitcher and turns it slowly, watching the thick flow of cream.

With one donut gone and the first half of the second in his mouth he looks at the girl for the first time. 'Yes?' he says. Of course he knows there's no reply she could make; she's there to bring the food and be humiliated. She stands at his desk, masking with her smile the nausea that has taken over her body, especially her stomach and groin.

'Yes?' he says again.

She smiles and pats her hips.

'I've brought you your coffee.'

He looks at her remembering his hand over her leg, his mouth at her breast. Beneath her dress everything is in place.

'That's all for now Miss Smith, incoming calls may be put through.'

Korsoniloff remembers for Tonker. Remembers the feel of her body, the taste of her genitals, the gasp of relief at climax. But no, Tonker couldn't come to her. He would sit regally in his chair and demand that his pants be taken off without any motion on his part. Tonker-Buddha, the bottom sphere of his belly exposed, his genitals half-covered, sits ready to be worshipped. Miss Smith is amazed. Shocked. Delighted. Awed. Bow down, his eyes say to her. She does, moving towards him. But then she stops. Vibrations of repulsion start her shivering. Communion with Tonker must be from a distance. She lies face down on the carpet and peers, past his garters and through his knees, at the holy irridescence.

'Holy cow' she says.

Tonker smiles benignly.

'Holy cow' she says and says again and again. Tonker

keeps smiling and when her awe has washed over her she assists him on with his pants and leaves him with his coffee and two and a half sugar-glazed donuts. He can now finish his repast and continue with the day's work.

Korsoniloff spinning uncontrollably out of balance nauseated by dizziness, nausea through his whole body. I have to vomit

XVIII

Tonker finally came to my place around seven. His task, as it turned out, included a few surprises for me.

'Now look Korsoniloff goddamit—'

It seemed I had received, for Tonker is an extraordinary man, an extraordinary benevolence. The idea had come to him when he originally visited me in my cell. Perhaps he had had some unconscious intuition of Korsoniloff's bereavement. In remembrance of our friendship, I have fond memories of you André, he had decided to do me a favour—the least he could do after all—and give me a world.

His way is ever changing and ever manifest.

He had brought with him, and not as an afterthought, Gail, whom he thought should be present. She sat, during his discourse, with her usual calm—her face unmoved and unmoving.

Now Tonker, in a diminutive way, was one of a long tradition of philanthropists who exist outside the established order. His gifts are dubiously received. But there are compensations. A good pimp may be harassed by the law and hated by his clients but he has, irrevocably and with more certainty than any social worker, the knowledge that his works are indispensable. So with Tonker. Of course in Gail he was endowed with an unusual commodity. Her lack of emotion was not, he admitted, a characteristic which he encouraged or which had resulted from her service to him. In fact it was a challenge. One of her many natural attributes which it would be his pleasure to destroy.

It was a bet. A straight bet.

See, she said she never got involved.

Like term life insurance. You bet the company that you will die within the next five years.

So I put it to her that she would be the perfect hostess.

You bet against yourself but that's no problem for a true gambler.

So with Tonker and Gail. He was betting she would break. If he won, he would lose, since the challenge would be gone. If he lost, however, he won, for he was still in the game. For Gail the prime goal was to perpetuate the game since, as her inducement to play, all her possible (within reasonable limits) material wants were satisfied by Tonker. In return for this inducement she was to do whatever Tonker told her to do.

What if she resigns? Gets a job? Falls in love? Gets married?

Tonker delightedly explained that he had considered these risks. But they were, in his estimation, counter-indicated by Gail's character. In fact, they were the point of the bet. She would not get a job, because she was too lazy to work and too confident to have to escape him. Second, he held up a finger still greasy from the afternoon's donuts, she would not fall in love and live happily ever after because she was incapable of happiness. She knew this herself and had no need of being told by him. Were she to attempt such a thing it would be certain to end up miserably for her and so she never would. Admittedly there was always the remote possibility. But that was a chance he was willing to take.

At this point Gail, who had neither looked at me nor avoided my eyes during Tonker's explanations, excused herself to go to the bathroom. Tonker, with a satisfied look, watched her leave the room. It was almost as if he knew that if she wasn't going to kill herself this time—and certainly she didn't seem upset—it was just a matter of waiting.

Is she really beautiful Korsoniloff? She really is isn't she?

Sure.

Does she enjoy it? Does she pretend to enjoy it?

Sure.

He had once made a similar arrangement with another woman but it hadn't worked out. After two weeks she had called the whole thing off and gone home to her parents.

Home to her parents, he said.

After that he probably wouldn't have tried it again if Gail hadn't come along. It was at a party, she was sitting beside someone. I'd know his name but he couldn't remember it, he was obviously on the make and she, the cat, was pretending to be the mouse. It was so obvious, she was doing it so publicly, he couldn't resist cornering her, taking her to a restaurant, and making a proposition. His original intention was that she be his mistress but when she refused he expanded the terms.

Gail came back into the room and sat down. Tonker looked at her possessively and smiled. Gail, without defiance, smiled back and then asked me for a cigarette. I gave her one, took one for myself, and offered one to Tonker. He refused and pulled out some lifesavers instead.

It was a beatific scene, really. The three of us sitting there, smoking and chewing and not saying anything. We all, for our various reasons, felt pretty good. Tonker was contemplating the inevitability of his victory, Gail was looking at a magazine she'd found on the floor, and I was enjoying the certitude that Tonker had so misjudged Gail that it would be years before he suspected anything.

But Tonker hadn't finished. Having anticipated, as he put it, the consummation of information that had taken place, he had brought along a little surprise. He opened his briefcase and pulled out a bottle, apricot brandy, and three glasses.

It is more blessed to give than to receive.

He looked towards Gail and pointed with his eyes to the bottle and glasses. She went into the kitchen with the glasses, rinsed them, and set them on the counter beside the sink. Then she came in and got the bottle, took it into the kitchen and poured the drinks. She brought in mine and Tonker's, then hers. Tonker waited until she was seated before raising his glass in a toast.

To truth, he said and drained his glass. Gail and I drank with him as he refilled his glass. It was kind of him to have remembered that I was a professor of philosophy. Tonker leaned back and surveyed the room. He looked at me sleepily and then looked at Gail. She sighed gently as his eyes closed and his head sank back into the chair.

Let's go, she said. Tonker was asleep.

It was the kind of warm summer evening that reminds you of other warm summer evenings so we drove about, each of us enjoying all the summers we had known. After a while we ended up at the reservoir and got out of the car to walk. We climbed a hill and looked down into the ravine. It was a perfect night and I wondered if the perfect thing to do would be to ask Gail to marry me. I lay back on the grass and imagined us living in Rosedale in a three-storey house with two kids and her sports-car. I would walk to and from the university—maybe sometimes she'd drive me—and at night we'd get high and look at picture books. Sometime I would take her back to Mikhail and Bess, they would like her, and take her for a walk on the beach. Since we had nothing to say to each other we wouldn't talk very much but that wouldn't be a great disadvantage. We have other ways to pass the time. We might even get to know each other. Every few weeks, maybe once a year, we would have Tonker to dinner. He would bring gross presents for the children who wouldn't be able to call him Uncle Alex but would welcome his visits nonetheless. They would make him get down on the floor with them and push around their toys. Gail, with utmost kindness, would finally tell them that it was time to go to bed and then, shortly after, tell Uncle Alex it was time for him to go home.

Gail was lying on top of me, her hair brushing against my face. Through the strands I could see the moon veiled and diffused, her eyes bright, the skin beneath them absolutely smooth and clear and looking through her hair I didn't see her lips move when she said that I didn't know what was happening but I answered anyway saying no I didn't. But I knew she would never tell me about her childhood in Saskatchewan or Vancouver or North York and that she would never tell me about the time, after her grade thirteen exams, that she was out at a party with the school football hero and finally lost her virginity or was it at a college dance because it didn't matter.

Her fingers were cool against my face and they melted into her particular curious silence. A silence that was itself mute that said nothing outside itself and reflected only that she had nothing to say but I was wrong for after a while she said that there was something else which was that we could keep seeing each other after tomorrow which was something she had known a long time ago and with that something in me let go, floated away to be absorbed somewhere else or maybe just to be taken into the diffused light that was now blinding me with my tears magnifying the nothing she started whispering my name over and over whispering my name into my ear whispering andré korsoniloff andré korsoniloff andré korsoniloff I listened hypnotised by the softness of her voice and breath which pulsed with the syllables of my name over and over washing the sound running the syllables indistinguishably together drowning me

When we got back to Tonker he was sitting in my chair where we had left him, reading some papers from his briefcase and sipping apricot brandy. He looked at us unperturbed and asked me if Gail had said she would marry me.

No, she said and took the empty glasses to wash them. When she came in to get Tonker's he asked me if I was prepared for the trial tomorrow.

Gail finished packing the glasses into the briefcase and helped him into his jacket.

See you at ten, he said. Sweet dreams.

XIX

The mirror informed me of my readiness. Eyes sunk
tragically into their sockets, I stared out remorselessly at myself. The skin over my cheekbones was dry and taut. I was
extra careful not to cut myself shaving. Staring into the mirror

Korsoniloff stalks his shadow pin-up remembrances of
past time, dissolving the convulsion to the linear

At the carotid vein, if there was an opening at that
place it could spill and overflow. Suicide on white porcelain;
the fastest most painless way for the man obsessed by order.
The vein would pump out with the heart

May I?
By all means.
Your turn to curtsy and my turn to bow.
No, let's do it the other way.
Come on.
You pretend you're an alligator and I'll be the swamp.
That's silly.
Alright, you think of something.

Alright. You be the buildings and I'll be the road.
Then what?
When? Oh, I don't know, we could see what happens.

Comes to a secretgreen garbagebag holds it up translucent
but when he goes to open it it has no insides and closed no
outside. Drops the gone bag

The complete plan would include calling emergency and
leaving the phone off the hook. By the time they got there the
blood would have stopped flowing and they would have a
relatively neat corpse to deal with. Of course that's assuming
the possibility that they might be squeamish. That might not
be justified. On the other hand, what if there was a new person
on the job? He probably would be. Even if the bleeding hadn't
stopped you'd be sure to be dead by then. At least I think so.
Nothing would be so humiliating as to commit suicide and
then be found alive. That would be a real *faux pas*.

Korsoniloff stopped to lean against a treetrunk. His jaw
flexed working sprucegum. As he rested he looked

Boy if anyone ever finds out.
So what if they find out?
You'll see so what if they find out you'll see then alright.
I don't care.
Neither do I. I guess. I don't care what but they just never
better that's all.
I guess you're right.
Hurry up then.

To see a darkform in the brightness but his hiding places
are lighted out, disappeared, so he moves towards it pushing

the light ahead of him to filter out the movement then running
flatout soles flapping flatout towards
Korsoniloff
Oldwoman passing collecting Korsoniloff stops to ask her
has she seen   She looks at him the skin beneath her eyes
soft and young and her eyes alive till the surrounding age
seeps through tracking the skin and
There are strange electric sounds oldwoman are they old
or new?
Saying nothing her eyes breakthrough again he looks in
to see a mountain collapsing   melted of its own weight sliding
down to its lava base   the peak drops emulsified   in time
unable to catch up
She looks away and continues on her path organised around
herself
Oldwoman is there something you're not telling me? She
glances facelessly at Korsoniloff and starts to
Hey Oldwoman you can't leave
No you can't. Winchester in the crook of his arm Korsoniloff shifts the weight to his hand kneeling on the path   his
knee in the damp bringing his left hand up under the barrel,
hot inside so when his wide open eyes confirm the intersect
he squeezes
All over everything is all over   bones and fragments   exploded she didn't just collapse   it's everywhere   Korsoniloff
wipes his hands on his jacket covered with it feels a piece on
his face   in his hair in the hollow of his throat brings it all
up over and over

Shouldn't have done that
No you shouldn't have done that
What are you going to do What are you going to do now?
Don't know.

101

I pressed the button for eleven.

There was a woman in the elevator watching me chew the gum. Her tongue ran back and forth between her lips. Want some?

No I was looking at your eyes.

My eyes? What's wrong?

They look friendly.

Tonker's secretary showed me into his office. Gail was already there, smoking and flipping through a magazine.

Tonker was eating jelly donuts. Watched me sit down. He was all set to put me at ease.

Relax Tonker, I said.

Very funny.

I trust you're prepared.

As for the dead man's float, anyone could learn that in a few minutes.

Well, said Tonker, we'll be on our way then.

XX

$100 or 14 days. I paid.

We went out into the corridor afterwards, the five of us, to stand and exchange pleasantries. Presently it got boring. Marie was very gracious and devoted to Harold, who was even more bored than I was. I stared at Marie for a time but her face was inaccessible. I felt Gail's hand on my back. We all excused ourselves and each other.

University Avenue in the summer. It was very hot and dusty and everyone looked busy.

Once Marie had lifted her eyes and looked at me in an amicable way. Old friends. I looked for the tiny flecks but couldn't see them. Perhaps she grew uncomfortable.

I walked over to Bay Street and found a small restaurant. The breakfast special was over but I ordered it anyway. It was the bacon I wanted. Bacon and orange juice and coffee. I had nothing to think about. Nothing to do but eat breakfast.

Summer. Everything seems to happen in the summer. When I went home last August Mikhail told me about the day Anna drowned. We were swimming; it was late July. Or rather we weren't swimming. She didn't know how and I was too young. She had taken me for a walk that morning. Mikhail must have

been doing something around the house—we always had some
sort of garden in the summer. We were standing on the dock—
I dove off it hundreds of times later though of course I
didn't remember anything at that point. Startled to be in
such a precarious place—I must have been afraid of water—I
ran to her for safety.

When they found us I was alone on the dock. I don't
remember any of it.

The funeral was the following day. Bess, it turns out,
stayed with me at the house.

When you were young you used to like to stand at the
window watching the snow flurries. And if it was the week
before Christmas you would watch for the postman too.
Wondering what he might be bringing you.

When I was in London. It was a small restaurant, fish and
chips with unlabelled sauces on the tables and your tea is
served with milk automatically. A clever young lady in a
smart tweed coat sat down unusually beside you perhaps to
pass the time of day or noticing the king-size cigarettes or
maybe even just to read your paper, you recognised her but
couldn't speak and rushed out leaving cigarettes newspaper and
unpaid bill which embarrassed

So every year we packed some of your presents and mailed
them to you from the post-office signed Santa Claus. Do you
remember the sled? Mikhail built it you were so disappointed
because there were no good hills but eventually you played
with it on the road. Jimmy Jarvis the butcher's boy taught
you to fish and who knows what else, picked you up every
Saturday morning and you both bicycled with the lunches
packed and always came back with something

And though she tried to get you to play or at least
talk you wouldn't see her or listen to her and insisted on
going up to your room alone

And so it went but of course I still didn't know what
they couldn't tell me.

I slid my finger into the bacon grease and licked it.
She smiled at me when I paid the bill. Tentative I smiled
backed. We laughed and I walked out into the heat.

Do your duty and let the mounty get the bounty

The hermit remembers his life for a while but finally it
passes from his consciousness

in/out on/off and if you blow a fuse there's always
therapy or something

But that day was walking still moving and re-moving
tracking over the same territory but the repetition was external.
I felt the wind and moved easily in the summer heat a familiar
inset to the land.
I bought an apple.
Blew it on College Street where the core bounced off
a tin and landed full-view on the sidewalk looking very chewed.
Picked it up and carefully deposited it on top of a lunch
bag that could have been salvaged with perhaps a transplant
of the serrated edge.

Oh you were a very happy child you cried sometimes
but all children do and you laughed too you remember walking
to school with Mikhail but when you went away you seemed

to go through a difficult period we knew it wasn't just the work but things turned out fine and we know you like your job probably you'll be getting married one of these days

Yes they did, they did indeed though of course I didn't appreciate it at the time they did indeed

At Queen's Park there was time to lie in the sun. The heat contented me. Blades of grass to play with and inspect the seams. And the chopped-off tops healing themselves. I fell asleep. I woke up. There was time for everything.
When I got home I found a note from Gail inviting me to her place.

Did I do it or didn't I?
I still don't know. But I know I never will.

I was standing with Gail on her balcony. We had come to love each other in a metallic sort of way. Did I tell you she was a Pisces? There wasn't much to say—we looked at the city. We were facing each other; it was windy. She looked at me, started to waver. I reached out my hands to embrace her. There was something about the way I did it. I looked at my hands. They were pulsing from curved to flat. Flat/curve. Pull to push. Push to pull. I could see her falling. Feel her against me. My eyes were closed. My hands seemed to shrink. It was all too familiar. The traffic sounds merged to a steady rush. I felt the weakness of my arms and the unsteadiness of my own stance. The slightest tip of time could have upset my balance and sent me falling against her my hands still undecided.
I opened my eyes. Gail was watching some clouds. I put my hands in my pockets and walked inside.